CEMETERY TACOS
AND OTHER DELIGHTS

NORA B. PEEVY

ISBN: 978-1-68510-172-5 (trade paper)
ISBN: 978-1-68510-173-2 (ePub)
The Library of Congress Catalog Number has been applied for.

First printing edition: April 17, 2026
Published by Trepidatio Publishing in the United States of America.
Cover Design: Don Noble
Edited by Sean Leonard
Proofreading and Cover/Interior Layout by Scarlett R. Algee

Trepidatio Publishing, an imprint of JournalStone
1400 North Wood Rd.
Murphysboro, IL 62966

Trepidatio books may be ordered through booksellers or by contacting:
JournalStone | www.journalstone.com

PUBLICATION NOTES

"The Telling Place" won second place for the monthly writing contest hosted by **Fantasy Gazetter** online, 2008.

"Carnivorous Cows from Outer Space" first appeared in the **Oddville Press**, online, 2008.

"A Taste of Murder" first appeared in **Twisted Tongue Magazine**, 2010.

"The Witch of Fox Point" first appeared in **The Beyond: Stories Inspired by the Lucio Fulci Death Trilogy**, curated by Raffaele Pezzella, 2021.

DEDICATION

This book is dedicated to my family; my mother, Rosalie; my brother, Adam; and my deceased father, Richard, for always believing in me.

ACKNOWLEDGMENTS

I'd like to thank Carson Buckingham for being my first editor to take a look at this book. I'd also like to thank my mother, my brother, and my best friend, Cindy for being my constant cheerleading team and believing in me, and my three English professors, Peter Blewett, Mary Blewett, and Paul Friedman for all their wonderful classes, discussions, and exercises that brought me to this moment. And lastly, thank you to all my friends on Facebook through the years who have believed and supported me in the horror community. Without you this book would not have been written.

CONTENTS

CEMETERY TACOS
AND OTHER DELIGHTS

KNOCK, KNOCK

The first time I remember being sad was when my *abuela* died. I was almost five years old, and it was the month before my birthday, July. It was the first human death I experienced, but it wasn't my first experience with death. My first real memory of death was from the year before, the last summer we lived on the banks of the Milwaukee River in our two-story house with my yellow bedroom and a porch swing great for reading books while drinking lemonade, as the cicadas droned on in the withering heat. I spent most of my time playing alone outdoors or reading that summer, which didn't bother me. I had willow trees to climb and a river to crayfish hunt in, and there were so many things to do in the summer.

One of my favorite things was exploring people's yards. When I was a child, my world knew no boundaries; the entire neighborhood was my backyard and we all looked out for one another. My neighbors had all these spiders living on their front porch and I studied them spinning their webs in the evergreen bushes. I found pill bugs and threw their hard, round bodies into the spiders' webs. The spiders were extra plump that summer, even the males. I remember my first experience with death in their backyard because it was so strange. They had a wonderful garden bursting with fresh mint plants in the shade of the elms. I used to pick the leaves and roll them between my fingers. They smelled like snowflakes, icicles, and Christmas—winter. It was hot for June on this particular day and I was enjoying the cool shade of their yard when I spied their tortoiseshell cat, Peaches, creeping amongst the bushes by their air conditioner.

I went to coax Peaches from her hiding place and found a small, brown mouse lying still and flat behind the air conditioner, as if something sucked all the air out of the poor creature. There was no blood. I couldn't understand how Peaches could do this and very gently, I picked it up and carried it home, the screen door wheezing a tired sigh behind me as I entered our small kitchen. My mother was making frozen orange juice pops for me, my favorite summer treat to eat on the porch swing while reading a good book. She looked pretty in my favorite skirt of hers, the pink patterned granny square one she'd made on the sewing machine last spring.

"Mom, look what I found behind Janet's air conditioner. I think it's hurt. Can you fix it?"

My mother's eyes bulged as if I'd just shown her a chopped finger, not a poor, helpless mouse. "Francesca, you drop it right now! Go wash your hands." She held the mouse by its tail as far away from her as she could and marched me to the kitchen sink where she turned the water on hot enough to scald me, my skin as red as apples before I was through.

"If I ever see you picking up a dead animal again, you will be in the biggest trouble of your life, young lady. Now go play or read a book until your father gets home." I could only assume "dead" meant not moving, but I didn't know how long the mouse would remain still. Perhaps it was only a few days. And that was my first experience with death.

***

Sometimes I felt motherless. I spent so much time away from my mother in the summer. Then I wound up Knock-Knock, my imitation Snoopy that played "Rock-a-bye, Baby" and hugged him close under the protection of a giant pine tree, its boughs a welcome respite, a living tent to retreat from my older cousins. Aunt Rosalia lived ten minutes away by car and I spent half my time there because both my mother and father worked second shift for extra money when I was out of school. Aunt Rosalia lived in a nice neighborhood where only pleasant things were supposed to happen, but I wasn't that lucky. My aunt smelled like medicine and slurred her speech. She slept all the time and my Uncle Tony ended up caring for me most of the time. Uncle Tony was Aunt Rosalia's fifth husband. "She went through husbands like babies go through diapers," my mother used to say when she thought I was asleep.

One night, a terrible storm raged. The rain pounded the sunroom windows where my crib was as whips of thunder lashed the darkness, lightning erupting in the backyard. I dreamt I was a baby crawling over broken glass, the pink knees of my sleeper torn and bloodied. I cried out for my mother, but the only sound was the hum of the streetlights. All the windows in the homes were dark. A monster lurked behind every shadow and my breath hiccupped in my chest as I struggled to breathe, bubbles of snot popping from my nose. My hands stung like a thousand paper cuts from the glass shards embedded deep in my palm.

A loud *boom!* shook the windows and I woke up on the sofa sleeper, my muscles taut with fear. I screamed and looked around for Knock-Knock, but I couldn't find him. It was then the sunroom door opened, and I smelled the hot, heavy grease of fried potatoes that clung to everything my uncle wore.

"Knock, knock," he said, smiling as he handed me my trusty companion. And then he kissed me like my parents never kissed me and did other things I wanted to forget. A tiny part of me faded away on that sweltering summer night and all the nights that came after. "Ssh, it's a secret. Don't tell anyone," he said every time he buttoned his shirt and left.

I wondered if I would ever find my smile again. Knock-Knock, my steadfast companion, witnessed everything. He shared my secret, and I knew he would never tell. He would never tell anyone, and he let me cry in his fur and his lullaby sang me to sleep as my tears dried on my cheeks. He made the darkness tolerable. I knew he would never leave me. Not ever.

***

I'd just come back from one of my visits at auntie's when we learned my *abuela* died. Abuela Maria was mom's mother. She grew up on a farm and bore seven children. She was a devout Catholic; we all were devout Catholics, so how could God let this happen? I pictured *abuela* as still as the mouse; for how long she would be still, I did not know. Perhaps not exceedingly long at all, because *abuela* was the most devout of us all. She prayed all the time, even when she babysat for me. I was scolded for playing in only my Wonder Woman Underoos™. I was going to be just like Linda Carter when I grew up.

The day we found out about Abuela Maria we heard a knock at the door. Knock, knock. Just two. It sounded like other knocks, like the census people's knock or the Girl Scouts' knock. There was no way to distinguish a knock of sadness. There should have been a special knock for someone telling me my Abuela Maria died, but there wasn't.

Knock, knock.

"Mother's dead." Aunt Rosalia leant against the doorframe like a wilted flower, the drooping petals of her bun clinging to her neck in the humidity, her mascara smudged.

After those two words came the food; casseroles, pies and cakes, and gelatin fruit salads with tiny marshmallows, and tamales, and everything you could think of showed up at our door. Everything, but my Abuela Maria who drove a big old car the color of yellow cakes, her purse stuffed with butterscotch candies wrapped in crinkling cellophane. Food was the universal language of death. I ate my last butterscotch. I had been saving it for the morning of my sixth birthday. From then on, I always associated that sweet, buttery taste with death.

***

There was nothing comfortable about the funeral service. Mother dressed me in my navy dress with an itchy collar. My *abuela* didn't wake up to talk to me. I didn't know why she was as still as the mouse for so long. It had to be bad, though, because everyone was crying. Abuela Maria lay in a shiny box at the front of the church. My mother told me to sit straight. The cloying perfume of carnations, roses, and lilies made me gag. I tasted butterscotch in my throat, a once happy memory now soured. The pews, hard and made of knotted pine, made my butt hurt; but then a curious thing happened. Abuela Maria began praying on her rosary wrapped around her wrinkled hands, her fingers flitting like a hummingbird's wings over the black polished beads, faster and faster as she prayed. Abuela Maria was not dead like the mouse. I looked around to see if anyone noticed this, but everyone focused on the priest in the pulpit, so I stayed quiet, and a small spark of hope leapt in my chest. I smiled at *abuela*, but she simply kept on praying on her rosary. It was toward the end of the service when I realized *God* spelled backwards was *Dog*. I thought of Knock-Knock waiting at home for me because mother wouldn't let me bring him.

After the ceremony, Mom told me to say goodbye to Abuela Maria. I couldn't understand it. I didn't want to say goodbye. I shied away from the front of the church, but my mother dragged me to *abuela,* and I saw she was still again. I didn't want to kiss her cold, pale cheek, but mother made me. I swear Abuela Maria smiled at me, but no one saw but me. Mother and I drove to the cemetery with tall stones and people crying. There was green grass, the greenest green I had ever seen. The earth pulsed with the heat of the sun underneath my white sandals. I asked if *abuela* could be undead for a while, to come to my birthday party next month, but Mom said it didn't work that way. *Abuela* would be like the mouse and rest underground beneath the dirt in her metal box, until I saw God too. I didn't want to ever meet God because he took my Abuela

Maria from me. I swore I wouldn't, but I cried and cried. I wondered if *abuela* was afraid of the dark like me. Scared and alone.

I cried a river of hot tears, and my pillow became a soggy salt-stained pancake. I wound Knock-Knock's music box over and over, until I heard a sharp *ping!* He played no more. I mourned my friend clutched tight to my damp, sticky cheek and breathed in his familiar dry, dusty smell. I watched the yellow streetlights come on outside and heard the older kids' laughter as I finally fell asleep.

***

Throughout my childhood, I kept Knock-Knock by my side and I would try to wind up his music box, only to have the key snap back on my fingers. Perhaps a spring was broken inside Knock-Knock, but whenever I truly needed him, he would play his lullaby just once for me before silencing. I would try to wind him up again then, but he wouldn't play. I decided it was a miracle sent from Abuela Maria and her God. It was like the first appearance of Our Lady of Guadalupe in 1531, but I knew the church wouldn't send anyone to investigate a young woman's beloved childhood friend. I heard about a woman who sold on eBay a grilled cheese sandwich with Christ's image on it and there's a site called "Jesustortilla.com," but the church hasn't sanctioned either of these as official miracles. The church would say it's blasphemy to believe such a thing, but I don't care because I don't believe in them or they would have saved my *abuela* because surely, if anyone deserved a second chance at life, it was my *abuela* who worked every day on her hands and knees scrubbing other people's floors just so she could buy food for her babies.

***

I didn't have the heart to box up Knock-Knock with my childhood toys. Locking him away would be a cruel betrayal of love, so he held a prominent place on my heirloom dresser I inherited from my Abuela Maria. Sometimes, when my husband hit me, I'd take Knock-Knock down and wind him up. He would always play his song just once and I would cry and then an unexplained blanket of calm settled over my shoulders. When I got divorced, he sang for me every night for a week. It was like praying in church to me, listening to his music. I never thought to question who was making Knock-Knock whole again, until one day, I heard a knock at my apartment door.

Knock, knock. My doorbell was broken. My landlord hadn't fixed it in months. It was my baby sister, Carmen. I braced myself to remain stoic because I knew what she was here about. I imagined my heart as a castle under siege and drew up the iron drawbridge to protect myself, but when I opened the door of my East Side apartment and saw my sister's face streaked with tears, I started crying too. I tasted butterscotch on my tongue.

"Mother's dead."

My breath stuck like a lump of bread caught in my throat and we held each other as we both cried. And then we prepared ourselves for the glut of food that would pass through our door. We cleaned my only table, the one in the kitchen, moving unopened mail and unread magazines. The red retro dining booth looked as naked and vulnerable as I felt. I hadn't seen it that clean since moving in two years ago. We sat down with cups of lemon tea. We didn't know what to say to each other at first.

"Remember how she used to try to save gas by turning off her car and coasting downhill?" We laughed. "Or the time she caught us sneaking out to the high school dance and she nailed our windows shut?" We laughed some more and sipped our tea until it was gone. Then we cried. We just sat holding hands together in my kitchen while the ticking of the clock kept vigil over us, until the rest of our family came.

They came and left and before I knew it, my sister was leaving too with the only piece of Tupperware I owned and one or two pie plates. I drifted on a sea of leftovers by myself. With my Persian, Champagne, by my side, I plowed through a plate of homemade lemon bars that wouldn't fit in my fridge. I didn't want them to spoil. The carton of milk in my fridge had soured, so I hunted down my only clean drinking glass for water and fished my last sleeping pill out of the Cookie Monster cookie jar. And then I padded off to bed.

The sheets were cool and my skin clammy. My furry therapist lay against me, purring. Knock-Knock rested on my other side. I ran my fingers through Champagne's silky fur, finding a few small knots I vowed to brush tomorrow, if I could muster the spirit. The ceiling fan murmured above us. It was the witching hour—midnight. Or was it *the wishing hour*? Perhaps it was both. *Time to make a wish.*

"Mom and Abuela Maria, if you're there, please let me know." And then I wound up Knock-Knock in the dark and listened.

THE TELLING PLACE

Logan floated weightless above his bed. He saw his head resting on the pillow and the stars reflected above him on the ceiling, so close, he could lick them. A giddiness flowed through his body, light, airy, and electric, as he pivoted; marveling at how different his room looked from this vantage point. This was what it was like to be a superhero.

He reveled in the power rushing through his arms and legs, a bolt of adrenaline slammed into his chest. His heart catapulted, and Logan struggled to find his voice, but it froze, locked away in an icy cage in his throat. Sweat pooled on his brow.

"N-no."

He shook his head. Climbing up the bedroom ladder with grimy nails and rotting, putrid flesh, the zombies advanced in rows of two. With terrifying grimaces and festering pus-filled tongues, bloated and deep purple, they continued climbing until the first two crouched by his ear, and he could hear the gnashing of their teeth and feel the cold chill and sharp pain of their splintered nails scratching his cheek.

The scream trapped within him, built to a terrible crescendo, until he thought his head would burst and explode into bits of gore dripping down the bedroom walls and soaking into his blankets.

Logan's fists crumpled the sheet in his searing palms as he tossed in bed. He watched the first wave of miniature zombies scale the mountain of his body. They licked their cracked lips and ran their diseased tongues over his skin before feasting on the fresh meat, gnawing his nose, his lower lip, his arms, and his legs. The wet ripping noises of Logan's flesh filled the night.

"No," Logan shrieked, and shot up in bed. He panicked, trying to focus on the dark shadows in his bedroom. His nightshirt was plastered to his back with sweat and his hair was a wet cap on his head as he reached with shaking fingers for the plastic emergency flashlight he kept under his pillow. The comforting click of the button calmed his heart as he shone the yellow beam on the model on his desk. It was just a model. Logan sighed. He willed his breath to slow as he counted the zombies. Twenty-six.

He adjusted the blankets, covered all his limbs, and listened to the dark. He could only hear the wind playing in the trees and Mr. Phil's cockapoo, Daisy, barking down the block.

One more check, he thought. He swept the beam of light over his model. Twenty-six. They were all there. All twenty-six of them. He thought he saw a blur of movement, and the curtains billowed with the breeze, bringing with them the moist scent of the river. He clicked off the flashlight, but, somehow, his boy mind knew it *could* be more than a dream, and he clutched his flashlight to his chest like a life preserver, prepared for a long night of unrest.

***

"Clarice." The snake heads addressed her with a chilly gaze. "Your next appointment is approaching." They flicked their slithery tongues over their scaly lips. Their red eyes slit like splintered rubies.

"Be quiet or I'll turn you four into a new pair of shoes. You're supposed to be a coat rack, for Hecate's sake."

The four snake heads snickered. Their dry scales rustled as they assumed the shape of four coat hooks; their eyes dulled and clouded over as their bodies and tails entwined to form the stand.

Ms. Sinclair peeked out the front window of her cozy reception room, rearranging on a cheery red table a rumpled collection of *Highlights* and *National Geographic.* The shadows from the windowpane did not fall across the crook of her nose or her face at all, odd and peculiar, but even more peculiar was the strange bone bird talisman around her neck, blinking and shrieking an ear-piercing squawk stifled by Ms. Sinclair's dry, bony hand.

Mrs. Martin and her son, Logan, blew in on a spirited door slam typical of a windy summer day in Wisconsin, the kind of day you're grateful for because as soon as you start to sweat from the cloying humidity, a big gust of wind tousles your hair and ripples through your shirt, fooling you into thinking it's not hotter than a witch's breath outside.

Mrs. Martin adjusted her pixie, scrunching and patting her reflection in the mirror by the door like an older diva. "Good afternoon, Ms. Sinclair."

"Good afternoon." She nodded to Logan. She noted his wariness as he placed his Red Sox cap on one of the coat hooks and ran a dirt-smudged paw through his hair. His skin smelled infused with sunlight and fresh air.

Mrs. Martin loved Ms. Sinclair. She felt Logan behaved so much better since he started coming here. Why, with just four visits he already said things like "Yes, Mom" and "thank you." Last Saturday, he cleaned his room without her asking. She made a note to call and thank Trudy Jenkins for the referral. The Telling Place was a wonderful resource for parents past the end of their rope and hanging on by two fingers. It was homey with all the knickknacks and mismatched furniture. It reminded her of Granny.

"Logan, what are you staring at, dear? Come have a seat."

"But Mom—"

"I said come have a seat." Mrs. Martin patted the crazy-quilt patterned couch, fingering a whimsical painted giraffe with her other hand. The wooden giraffe sneered at the unsuspecting mother.

Ms. Sinclair frowned at the giraffe as the tips of her fine silver brows drew together. They were one of her prettier features.

"But Mom," Logan said again as his plump body. sweat-drenched after baseball practice, plopped down on the couch, "I swear one of those snake heads blinked at me."

"Really, Logan." Logan recognized his mom's tone from previous fights at home—the "don't push it further" tone. Her denim eyes flushed with embarrassment. "Do you see what I put up with, Ms. Sinclair? Kids and their imaginations." She laughed an uncomfortable laugh as she rumpled her son's ginger hair.

Still frowning, Clarice risked a quick peek at her coat rack in the corner. A black snake tongue flicked the air. Clarice crossed the room with the afghan from the back of her rocking chair in her grasp. "We'll just cover this so it doesn't bother you, Logan." She smiled at him with perfect, straight teeth, pinching the nose of the offending serpent between two iron fingers. As she draped the coat rack with her blanket, she said in a firm voice, "Just you behave now, or I'll be frying you up for the cat's supper later." A marmalade cat poked her pink nose out from behind a collection of dusty tomes on the bookshelf, grinning with glee and licking her whiskers. With her grandmother smile perched upon her lips, Clarice turned to reassure Logan. "All better," she said as she sat in her rocking chair across from them.

Logan studied her face. He heard dry scales rubbing against each other in her voice. He didn't like The Telling Place. It was a place you went to tattletale on someone, and Logan knew other kids didn't like tattletales. It went against the kid code. He didn't like Ms. Sinclair, either. As his mother would say, he couldn't put his finger on it, but he knew something wasn't right. Something wasn't right at all. He glanced again at the rack, swallowing his nervousness, as he witnessed a serpentine movement from beneath the colorful afghan.

"So, Mrs. Martin, how are things at home with Logan this week?"

"They're going better." She smiled at Logan. "Why, I don't know what you and Logan talked about Ms. Sinclair, but Logan's attitude improved overnight. It's like magic." Mrs. Martin beamed brighter than a full moon night.

"Anything new?" Ms. Sinclair loomed closer to Logan like a dragon eyeing its prey.

"Well…" Mrs. Martin glanced at Logan and patted his chubby hand. "We have one problem."

"Oh?"

"Logan's been spending a little too much time on his models and not enough time on his grades. He got another failing grade in math this week."

"Logan, is this true?" Ms. Sinclair watched the boy flush a nice shade of red to match her coffee table.

"Yes." He hung his head and picked at a week-old scab on his knee.

"Why do you think that is, Logan?"

"I don't know." He shrugged his shoulders, conscious of Ms. Sinclair's crooked nose pointed in his direction. Could a woman like Ms. Sinclair be married? Could she have a family; a boy like him at home? No. She wasn't like his mom. He felt it in his gut.

"Maybe you'd feel more comfortable talking to Ms. Sinclair on your own, Logan?" Without seeing her son's panicked stare, Mrs. Martin stood and adjusted her purse strap on her shoulder. "I'll just do some shopping and be back in half an hour."

"Wait." Logan's heart jigged in his chest.

"Bye, son." She winked at him, and the red door closed with an ominous *click*.

Ms. Sinclair's eyes gleamed with voracious delight. "Now we're alone, Logan, and we're going to have a little chat about responsibility and doing one's homework. Give me your hand."

Logan felt his stomach riding hot acid waves as he touched Ms. Sinclair's hand. The last time he'd done so, he'd felt the cold of metal in winter and smelled a rank beast. He'd also heard the sharp snap of a dried turkey wishbone and tasted stale cinnamon. This time he tried to focus on

Shep's happy smile; his pink dog tongue hanging lopsided out of his mouth.

Ms. Sinclair sensed Logan's fears. She pushed past the grinning, childhood image of the idiot dog not even fit to carry fleas and searched deeper into Logan's mind. She saw a blue painted room with plaid-clad bunk beds and a spaceship nightlight. Her tongue flicked over her lips, and her fingertips itched with anticipation, as she homed in on a secondhand desk strewn with tubes of colored paint, model glue, and assorted paintbrushes held in an old Jif peanut butter jar.

She grasped her bird whistle until Logan saw her knuckles turn gray, and he closed his eyes, trying to hold onto Shep's face. He wanted to pull his hand away from hers, but primordial instinct told him it was better to remain still and not to wake whatever beast lay slumbering behind Ms. Sinclair's eyes.

Ms. Sinclair stroked the whistle, feeling the bone warm and stir beneath her fingertips. She peered closer at the modeling table in Logan's room. "Now, Logan, you know you need good grades to get a good job someday?"

"Yes."

She saw a tiny zombie miniature on the table; its face drawn back in snarled agony as it carried a miniscule dagger in its fist. She smiled. "And you know you have to obey your parents, and that your mom wants you to get good grades?"

"Yes."

Ms. Sinclair focused on the graveyard model displayed on the desk. The undead locked limbs with the living as they crept, staggered, and clawed their way from their graves. They shuffled around toppled gravestones and out the rusted cemetery gate with their lips pulled back in menacing howls and wild hunger in their eyes. She stroked her whistle. "Then you'll work harder at your homework? To do your homework before your models?"

"Yes." Logan felt a viscous slug monster crawling up his arm into his mouth, probing with its wet foot. He spat and opened his eyes, startled. Yanking away his hand, he noticed nothing there, but tasted vile brine in his mouth. "Sorry." He wiped the palms of his hands on the front of his *Star Wars* shirt. "I thought a bug flew into my mouth." He blushed, realizing he sounded foolish.

"That's quite alright, Logan." Ms. Sinclair glanced out the window. "Your mother's back."

The red door opened, and Logan heard the faint tinkle of the ice cream truck outside.

"Ready?"

"Yes." He hugged his mom.

"Did everything go okay, Ms. Sinclair?"

"Yes, it did. I'll see you the same time next week."

"Thank you."

"Goodbye, Logan."

"Bye."

Ms. Sinclair waited until their tomato red car turned the corner on Wabash at the light, before she raised her whistle to her lips.

***

"Mrs. Hammond, I assure you hypnotism is an accepted form of therapy for children, proven to show significant results overnight." Clarice smiled at young Johnny, who sat on the floor crashing two Hot Wheels into each other on the braided rug.

"You're going to die in a fiery pit of burning hell!"

"See what I mean, Ms. Sinclair? It's not normal—the aggression he displays. And the fighting with his sister at home has escalated." Mrs. Hammond rubbed her weary eyes. "I don't know what to do anymore. I'm working such long hours at the hospital. I can't put him in an afterschool program with his behavior like this."

"I'm sure I'll be able to help you, Mrs. Hammond. It's good you brought him to me. If you'll give me a half hour alone with Johnny, I promise you'll see results before his next session."

"Fine." Mrs. Hammond was almost out the door already. She needed no prodding to escape from her son for half an hour.

Clarice stopped her in the vestibule. "Mrs. Hammond, if you don't mind my asking, where did you hear about my services?"

"From Logan's mother."

"Oh." Ms. Sinclair smiled. "Enjoy your time alone. Most mothers do." She grinned.

As Ms. Sinclair closed the door, Mrs. Hammond saw the small bird talisman squirm against the old woman's purple blouse. *But no, it couldn't be.* It was just her imagination.

"In a pit of fiery burning hell!"

"Yes, Johnny, some day we will all die in a fiery pit of burning hell, but in the meantime, why don't you come over here, and talk to me for a minute." Clarice stared at the boy on the rug and followed his gaze to the painted wooden chest on the opposite wall. *Well, if he won't listen to me, we'll just get his attention, won't we? The little maggot.* Clarice glowered as her fingers stroked the bone bird whistle hanging from her waddled neck.

Johnny sat mesmerized by the wooden chest; his arms remained poised over the rug with his cars suspended in mid-crash. The chest boasted a jungle scene carved in bas relief and painted in electric blues, magentas, neon greens, and psychedelic yellows. Lions, giraffes, monkeys, parrots, and serpents capered and danced under leafy umbrella palms with tall men. The greens were so lush, Johnny could taste the sweet, cool juice from their stems. As he reveled in the details of the scene, the figures shivered and quaked. One lanky man raised a machete and decapitated a giraffe. Its yellow body ran bright crimson with blood. Johnny looked away from the gruesome scene as animals fled shrieking and squealing into the jungle. He clambered for the warm safety of the couch by Ms. Sinclair's rocking chair and wrapped the granny square afghan around his quivering shoulders.

"You w-wanted to talk to me, Ms. Sinclair?" Why couldn't Johnny see her pupils? She didn't have any. He shivered, pulling the afghan tighter around his body.

"Yes, I wanted to talk with you, Johnny. Just a friendly talk. Nothing bad. Give me your hand," Ms. Sinclair beckoned, and slid her rocking chair closer to the couch.

Johnny knew that voice. It was the *lying* voice. It was the voice Dr. Martin used when he told Johnny the shot wouldn't hurt much or the voice Johnny's sister used, when she promised to take him to the park if Johnny left her alone for a while. It was a dark, bruised voice, the *lying* voice. Johnny didn't want to disappoint his mother again. He really didn't, so he gave Ms. Sinclair his left hand and squeezed his tongue tight against the roof of his mouth to keep from screaming.

"Close your eyes, Johnny."

He closed his eyes.

Clarice put her bird whistle to her wizened lips and blew once. A piercing squawk hurt his ears. He winced. "Tell me about your sister, Johnny."

Johnny's voice hung wasp-nest thin in the air. His eyelids fluttered. "I don't like her. She threatens to cut the heads off my G.I. Joes and steals my candy. She tells on me and gives me purple nurples."

"I see." As Clarice held the boy's soft, clammy hand, she saw a long-legged girl with a slender, coltish neck and a delicious, mischievous grin. "Is that why you beat her up?"

"No," he blurted. "She beats me up first."

"And how does that make you feel?"

"Angry."

"Keep talking." Clarice pressed deeper into the boy's consciousness, searching, searching for… *Ah yes, there it was.* She stroked her bird talisman again. It grew, simmered, and became malleable like the boy's hand.

When Johnny was younger, two, maybe three, his mother read him the story "Three Billy Goats Gruff." The long rickety bridge they crossed didn't frighten him and the troll with the nasty eyes didn't frighten him, but he hated the goats, even though they were the heroes of the story. They stank at the petting zoo his mom took him too as well. They ate your nametags and slobbered slimy spit in your hand, contaminating your body with germs, while flies buzzed around to bite their smelly legs. At night he'd gone to sleep, and the goats plagued him with their foul odor and their yellow eyes focused like lasers in the dark as they bared their brown stained teeth, their hooves tapping with anticipation. *Click, click, click.*

The boy was strong—almost too strong. He knew something was wrong. Clarice saw it written in his scrunched-up face, his mouth a shriveled raisin. She tasted his fear in the air, alkaline and scrumptious. Continuing to stroke her bird whistle, she said, "Johnny, do you remember the goats?"

"Y-yes." His grip on her hand could crush a drinking glass.

"When I say 'hippopotamus' and tell you to open your eyes, you won't remember my asking."

"'Kay." His lids fluttered and stilled. Johnny thought of the ballerina elephants in *Fantasia.* It must be the mention of hippos. He smiled.

"Hippopotamus. Open your eyes, Johnny." Clarice startled as her office door opened. Mrs. Hammond had returned with a bag of Einstein Bros bagels in her hand.

"Did you have a good talk?"

"Y-yes, Mom." He couldn't remember. *Odd.* He remembered a hippo or a dancing elephant. His tongue felt swollen, and his head felt thick like he'd been sleeping too long.

"Well, Johnny, you'd best get out of here and make the most of what's left of the daylight. It'll be dark before you know it." Ms. Sinclair grinned.

"'Kay."

"Johnny, why don't you wait for me in the car? We'll go get a Happy Meal after I finish talking with Ms. Sinclair."

"'Kay."

She waited until he safely rounded the corner. "Anything I should know about?"

"I think you'll see a remarkable improvement, Mrs. Hammond. Johnny's hypnosis went very well, better than expected. We got to the root of the problem, but if you do have any episodes at home before our next visit, just say 'hippopotamus.' That's Johnny's magic word when things get out of control."

"What's a magic word?"

"Just a little reminder for Johnny to behave." Clarice patted Mrs. Hammond's shoulder.

Mrs. Hammond, who felt like a goat, which was very strange, saw a goat reflected in Ms. Sinclair's eyes. And her feet buzzed like they'd fallen asleep. *Weird.* "See you next week then, Ms. Sinclair. And thank you for seeing us on such short notice. You're an angel."

Or a devil, Clarice thought. "Goodbye, Mrs. Hammond." She watched them pull away, stroking her bird whistle with an idle hand.

***

"Rat breath!"

"Pizza face!" Johnny sneered at his sister, for he knew how sensitive she was about her skin.

Mae snarled as her fists hammered into Johnny's back. Johnny fell to the floor, unable to breathe, his back on fire. He scrabbled backwards.

"I'm gonna beat your butt, you lil booger!"

"Not before I kick your ass!" Johnny leapt to his feet like a video game fight contender, fists drawn for action.

"That's enough! Stop it, you two, before I give you both a reason to cry." Johnny's mom looked angry enough to split him in two.

"I'm tired of her picking on me all the time." Hot rivulets of tears gushed down Johnny's cheeks.

"Hippopotamus," Mrs. Hammond spluttered over her tea.

Johnny's leg muscles weakened and he fell, hitting his chin on the floor.

"Think you're so hot now, pipsqueak?" Mae kicked him in the kidney.

Johnny whimpered. Mae's face morphed into an ugly, hairy, rank-smelling goat with a scruffy beard and wild bloodshot eyes. A frenzied bleating spilled forth from her mouth. He covered his ears with his fists to block out the terrible sound.

"'Next time it's gonna be worse. You can count on it." Mae stood over him, but all Johnny heard was the demonic bleating of the goat.

The bleating! Johnny couldn't take another second of it. He slammed his fists against his ears, hoping to beat out the noise as he sobbed, curled up on the floor. "I'm sorry, Momma! I'm sorry! I promise!"

His chest heaved as he sneaked a cautious glance at his sister through a curtain of tears. Mae was his ugly, mean older sister again. He hugged his arms tight to his chest, the tears wracking his body, as his mother knelt beside him, smoothing her cool hand over his burning forehead. "Sssh…"

***

"What do you think, kitten," Clarice asked the marmalade cat cleaning itself on the braided rug. "Do you think we'll have any new clients today?"

The cat paused and then continued cleaning, not even looking at her. Clarice sipped her tea, enjoying the robust mint flavor. She turned as the bell above her door tinkled. A pretty middle-aged mother and her blonde daughter stood in the doorway.

"Hello, I'm Ms. Sinclair. And you are?"

"Mrs. Richie, and this is Samantha."

Samantha found the woman smelled musty, like old books from her grandma's trunk in the attic.

Ms. Sinclair extended her hand to Samantha. "Hi there, sweetie."

"Well, shake her hand, Samantha."

Not wanting to, Samantha took Ms. Sinclair's ancient, dry hand in hers. She felt a slithering beneath the old woman's skin. She did not like The Telling Place. She did not like The Telling Place at all.

A TASTE OF MURDER

I leaned into the open car window with a casual grace and a coy grin. "Can I get a ride?" My breath smelled sweet as bubblegum as I flicked my long hair over one lean, tanned shoulder, using the gifts my mother gave me. Men—they're so easy to manipulate. Show this one a little leg, show that one a little boob, and they salivate like the dogs they *really* are. This one was a special breed of sicko.

"Sure can." He leaned over to open the door for me, noting the dust on my boots with a small grimace as he watched me fold my lanky frame onto the hot, vinyl seat. I shifted my legs for his benefit, positioning my cowboy boots around a worn and faded black backpack. The stale fug of the pine tree hanging from his rearview mirror, mixed with the Old Spice, showed this guy hadn't had a date in decades. A trickle of sweat ran down my neck and settled between my breasts, leaving a wet spot on my red babydoll tee. I let out a long sigh and gathered my hair from my sticky neck, snapping a black band off my slender wrist with my fingers, long and agile as a pianist's and my nails painted a blazing red. He was like my husband—a lying, mangy cur who tricked me into eating those damn pomegranate seeds, but no matter. I knew his type, looking for a cheap thrill with a wild finish, coveting something he'd never owned—*me*.

"So, what's your name?" I squinted into the sun as I licked my lips and flipped down the visor on my side.

"Everybody calls me Earl." He tried to focus on the writhing snake of blacktop ahead, a river of green cornfields streaming past as he drove, but I could tell his fingers hungered for fresh flesh. Time limped along on a broken foot for poor, desperate Earl. He'd been trapped between a scorched piece of highway and the baking sky all morning and afternoon. I could tell he thought he had a new friend.

I laughed—the sharp, staccato rhythm of a pair of high heels on pavement—and snapped my gum, slouching lower in my seat and putting my dusty black boots on the dashboard, exposing another inch of oiled, tanned thigh in my tight Daisy Dukes. "I've never met any Asians named 'Earl.' You're all named 'Lee Chung' or something." I snorted, stomping my boot heel on the dash, positive that would really get Earl's blood a-boiling.

He frowned at my boot. I'd pegged him for a control freak, all right. "I'm a first generation American. I don't need an Asian name." He paused, the corner of his mouth twitching, as I tapped my toes on the dashboard. Like bricks, his words fell heavy and uncomfortable from his mouth. "Will you please take your boots off my dashboard?" I lowered my boots to the floor with a rebellious *thump!* Giddy as a schoolgirl picking daisies, I stared out the window. A flock of red-winged blackbirds rose in a blue arc of sky. I could practically see the roots of Earl's black hair burning crimson with anger. He admired the curve of my nose. *An exemplary specimen of Roman beauty*, I heard him think. I could hear everything men thought, being born from a Goddess. I smelled my own body heat. The candy apple scent of my hair made him smile again. He turned his attention back to the road. "What's your name?"

"Persephone." My name hung like a ripe red-orange fruit between us in the humidity. I rocked my left boot back on its heel, my long fingers splayed in delicate grace across my knee.

"And you're laughing at me?" His skinny frame shook as he chuckled. Then he grew quiet. His shirt slick with sweat, he shifted his weight in the car seat, the vinyl chafing and burning his skin. I sensed he suffered from a sharp kink in his neck, like someone twisting a screwdriver into it, and I wanted to twist it a little further, but slowly, for my own amusement. Mind you, I hadn't always been this way, but so the seasons make the girl, and the girl makes the seasons.

"My mother was the original hippie." I rolled my window down further, enjoying the breeze.

Earl watched patches of sunlight flickering over my face as I spoke, my arm draped out the window. "You talk about her in the past tense. Is she..?"

"Oh, she's not dead. She lives out of state. I visit her almost every summer."

"Where does she live?"

"Mt. Olympus, Washington. I'm hitching my way there. Do you like my shirt?" *Demeter Does Zeus* stretched taut over my breasts in bold white lettering, cracked with wear and washing. I could hear his cock stirring in his pants. *Sooey, boy! Come and get it!*

"It's a nice top."

"Even though the shirt's a little worn, I still wear it because it reminds me of home." A tiny, sweaty, blonde wisp clung to the nape of my neck. It was hot enough to fry Hades in here! Hmm… A nice thought. I would have to come back to that one at a later juncture. "Don't you have air conditioning?" I leaned forward to fiddle with the dials on the dashboard.

"Please, don't do that." Earl placed his hand on top of mine. I grinned, flashing my oh-so-cute dimples with an impish, irresistible wiggle of my brow. I did not remove Earl's hand from mine as I popped a huge pink bubble in his face, wrapping my other hand around Earl's, feeling the warm curve of his palm in mine. "You don't work with your hands much, do you?" I stared at his thin fingers, fine-boned as a blue heron's wing and soft as a child's.

I watched Earl recall a ghost memory of the last girl who held his hand, the vintage pinup pouting lips, and the taste of cinnamon kisses on his tongue stealing his thoughts. He swallowed, forcing himself to speak. "I'm an accountant." I saw the corner of his mouth twitch as he took his hand away from mine. *Liar.* I decided to turn up the heat a notch and I opened his glove compartment, rummaging for a napkin and shuffling through a thick stack of maps banded together, vehicle registration papers, and a pair of black gloves causing my skin to scream on contact.

Earl's brow wrinkled and his upper lip twitched. He bit his tongue, frowning, as he leaned over to slam the tiny door shut. "That stuff's private. Understand?"

So he was a control freak and didn't want me in his private cesspool of filth. Hmmm… Well, I could give him something else to be mad about. Maybe he'd snap, and I could finish him off early, and be on my way. I pouted like a naughty debutante, spitting my gum into a Dairy Queen napkin, which I crumpled and tossed to the floor by my boot. "What do you think about that, Earl?" I leaned over, my breath hot and sugary in his ear. *That should stoke his engine a bit.*

From the corner of his eye, I could see him peeking down the front of my top. He shoved me back into my seat. "I think you should pick that up and put it in the trash bag. That's what I think about *that.*" He pointed to a small white plastic bag on the floor near my backpack.

"Fine." I sighed, pretending to be perturbed as I bent over to pick up the wadded napkin. "Are you this rude to every girl you pick up?" This was taking longer than I'd originally planned, but luckily for Earl, I was a persistent girl.

"Are you this rude to every man that gives you a ride?" I could see the internal struggle, how hard he willed his mouth to stop twitching, giving a stiff smile and a wink.

"No." My voice became muffled as I popped a cherry sucker from my bag into my mouth and put the wrapper in the trash bag with a slow deliberateness; my eyes locked onto his as I ground the trash bag beneath the pointed toe of my boot. It lay like a shriveled onion on the floor as I took my sucker out of my mouth, licking my red-stained lips, fully aware of the flirtation and relishing every minute of it. Reeling him in a little more.

Earl swerved around a small pile of brown fur in the road. "Rabbit."

"Plenty of those where that one came from." I popped my sucker back in my mouth.

Too much corn, I heard him think. *When will it ever end?* He checked his watch.

"Gotta be somewhere?" I knew where he wanted to be, but he wasn't going to get *there*. It'd be a cold day in hell before Charon even got in bed with me. Stealing me away from my family—the epitome of the brute cave dweller dragging his wife to his den by the hair, so unevolved and uneducated and unprepared to deal with the likes of me, just like my precious, naïve little Earl. But Earl thought he *could* get with me and after imprinting on those black leather gloves, I knew about his special plans for me.

"Nope." Earl shifted in his seat.

I stuck my hand out the window. "Did you ever see *Children of the Corn*?" My subtle wit was lost on Earl—sad there was no one to appreciate the reference. I'd take a standing ovation, but then, was sure I'd get one from Earl sooner or later. I stretched my hand farther out the window, trying to grab a stalk as we drove the deserted road. Every few miles, the black hat of a scarecrow popped up out of the monotonous green and blue landscape. You'd think I'd appreciate my mother's handiwork *more*, but *really*, if you've seen one cornfield, you've seen them all.

"Didn't see that flick." Earl scratched his chin.

"Too bad for you." I shifted in my seat.

He squinted at a wavering streak of red in the distance, drops of sweat rolling down his nose. "So, you watch scary movies often?"

"Oh, yeah." I shuffled my feet, stripping the last bit of sucker from the white paper stick with my two front teeth. A bright red stop sign sprung up from the pavement at the top of the hill, cornfields still pressing in on both sides of us. Earl inched to a stop and then scooted the nose of his car into the intersection. The loud angry honk of a semi blared down on us, the driver glaring and shaking his fist as he passed Earl's car.

"Shit, that was close." Earl's heart slumped somewhere around his knees.

"You were saying something about scary movies?" I beamed, relishing his discomfort and scratching my neck with a bored sigh. "Does your radio work?"

"Nope."

I stared out the window. Wasn't there a gas station anywhere in this godforsaken place? I'd been waiting on the road all day for Mr. Scumbag to show up; with my mother's gifts, I knew everything, being born from a Goddess, and my feet were sore, my back itched with sweat, and I could really use something for this companion headache. I wanted air conditioning, cold water, and vengeance faster than Paris Hilton could spend her daddy's money, but it didn't look like I had a chance in finding either for at least another hour. I scowled.

Earl checked the gas gauge: a quarter of a tank left.

"Do you have anything to read?" I peeked in the backseat, giving him a backside view of my Daisy Dukes. They crept higher as I rustled amongst empty paper bags and soda cans. Finally, I sat up victorious, my cheeks flushed and damp hair springing loose from my long ponytail like Medusa's serpents, a wrinkled newspaper in my hand. I settled down into my seat with my discovery, the toes of my boots resting on my pack with the newspaper smoothed across my tanned thighs. I scratched my throat and glanced down at the headline: *Midwest Mangler Strikes Again.* Meh! I already knew who that was.

"Any good news?" Earl turned left on County E. More cornfields welcomed us.

I watched the setting sun stain the horizon a deep red, the color of a blood orange's pulp. I wanted to kick the shit out of this poor excuse for a man. After Hades, I held little patience for wankers. "The Midwest Mangler killed some girl in Mayville this weekend."

"What a shame. How many young women has he killed? Is it twelve? That's the number I heard last night." He smiled. "He's probably going for lucky thirteen."

"Thirteen's my lucky number, Earl." I flashed him my absolute best Las Vegas showgirl smile as my fingers played over his thigh with sensual warmth, restraining myself from digging in with my nails and stripping his quads.

"Please, don't touch me." Earl peeled my fingers from his leg like he was peeling the skins of rotten fruit. He watched me. His cagey eyes caught the dying sun, a flash of blood flickering in muddy brown puddles.

So, he doesn't like to be touched, huh? I trailed a lazy "S" over my collarbone with my long red nails, my eyes roaming down to my inner thighs. As I sank lower in my seat, I let my legs fall open just a little bit, revealing smooth, tender skin. "I hope we can stop soon. Don't you, Earl?"

"Yes."

He glanced away from me, and I saw images of me writhing beneath him burned into the core of his vulgar mind. His mouth twitched as he leaned into the curve ahead.

A tiny gas station appeared around the bend next to a white clapboard house with red geraniums in window boxes. As we parked, an elderly man with a striking resemblance to James Earl Jones poked his head up from his newspaper at the counter. He eyed Earl with a dull, rheumy curiosity, his face dark in the window. It hadn't been washed since saddle shoes made a comeback in the 1950s. I arched my back like a cat, getting out of the car, bending over to grab my ankles and stretch, and for the old man's extra benefit I lifted my head up from the ground with a suggestive smile. My blonde ponytail cascaded over one shoulder as I held my ankles. The old Black man turned away from the ample view of my cleavage. Instead, he watched Earl pumping gas. He hadn't paid me much interest, but I knew he was a slavering rat like the rest of them. Most men were. That's why I'd gone into the exterminating business in my free time. Never again would I be a helpless victim, and a little vigilante justice could help my sisters in need too.

Earl finished pumping gas and headed inside. The little bell above the door tinkled as I entered, bringing a hot cyclone of air with me. I nodded to Earl at the register as he went to pay for the gas and wove through the short aisles, trailing lazy fingers across the glossy packages of gum. Eyeing the Red Vines licorice, I plucked another cherry sucker from a display tree, unwrapping it. I crumpled the waxy wrapper in my hand, wedging it between two rows of Juicy Fruit on the shelves and twirling a stray wisp of hair around a finger, a coquettish smile on my lips, walking over to Earl.

"You have to pay for that." The old man frowned.

Earl pulled two worn dollar bills from his wallet, leaning on the counter. "Keep the change, mister."

"Do you have a bathroom I could use?" My tongue was stained a deep cherry red.

"Out back." The old man slid the key attached to a battered piece of wood across the counter and I sidled out of the store, my boot heels clicking, the key jangling in my hand, and fully aware they watched me leave with hungry eyes.

***

I sat with my back against the clammy yellow tile. I tossed my red sucker on the floor by the toilet, my elbows resting on my knees as the doorknob turned. A cockroach scuttled past me, and I ground it into the tile with the toe of my boot, picturing Earl's face. The muggy air nuzzled like an eager kitten against my chest, lapping the breath from my mouth. I wrinkled my nose, overcome by the sweet noxious stink of old rose deodorizer and urine. The faucet dripped. I steadied myself for the encounter.

Earl stood in the sulfur haze of the overhead light in the bathroom, small white moths beating their frantic wings against its globe. He leered at me, his hands encased in his black gloves, and I flashed him a lynx grin, rising to run my red nails over my wrinkled Daisy Dukes.

"Hello, Earl." I sauntered to the tiny sink to splash icy water on my throat, my hips swaying, the droplets running down to my breasts, so many diamonds reflected in the light from the doorway. He rested his hands on the doorframe. "It's hot in here, isn't it?" A wave of bronzed hair tumbled around my face as I undid my ponytail. Flecks of gold flickered in my green eyes, and I swayed with the grace of a cat, my long brown legs shimmering.

Earl savored this moment, watching my ample chest rise and fall as I breathed. The slight tilt of my head beckoned him. The faint, moist smell of fertile earth clinging to the air around me whispered sunny childhood memories in his ear of running through gold-kissed fields under an autumn sky so crisp. He shook his head, focusing on my face in reverie. *Yes, Earl. I could conjure whatever images I wanted in your demented mind.*

I pulled the red top over my head, letting it drop to the floor. I stood there, my areolas large, the color of ripe pomegranates in the semi-darkness of the bathroom, the overhead light flickering and buzzing. My areolas lay like two half-moons, pleading for his kisses. "Come here, Earl." *Come here so I can kill you, Earl.* I grasped his gloved hands and pulled him toward me, steeling myself not to recoil from his tainted flesh. I envisioned myself as a sharp sickle eager to cut down his sheath, borrowing a little of my mother's legacy. He tore off his gloves and flung them to the floor. They crumpled like wilted flowers beneath our feet as he ran his fingers down my throat.

"Kiss me, Earl." *Kiss me so I can kill you, Earl.* I threw my head back, letting him taste me. The petrichor scent of my skin swelled, pulsing around him, calling him to me like a babe as I opened my mouth to him. His hands reached to cradle my face, my cheekbones finer than a dragonfly's wing. I tasted Red Bull and beef jerky and tried not to puke.

My strong arms encircled his waist. Around us the air sizzled with the reedy symphony of dry cornhusks grinding together. My body turned, entwining with his, pinning him to the tiled wall. As my hands stroked his chest, teasing his cinched belt, I gave him a pouty Marilyn Monroe smile.

I could feel the box cutter in his back pocket. Green tendrils of smoke snaked upwards, winding their wispy arms around us. Earl blinked, mesmerized. He sighed as my fingers stroked his stomach. I tore his shirt off like we were in a cheesy porno. Really, I wanted to tear his head off with my bare hands and use his spinal cord as the newest belt in my collection, but I had discipline after all these years on the road tracking down the slime of the earth. I would relish this moment like a fine wine and a box of chocolates—every girl's best friend.

"Are you happy, Earl?" I wriggled against him, undoing his belt, and stepped back, my hair glowing a luminescent gold, millions of fireflies entangled in my tresses. I saw him marvel at my transformation. He thought it was a hallucination. It didn't matter. Tendrils of green smoke twined around my torso as my eyes shone like a coyote's, two pinpoints of amber in the semi-darkness. While Earl watched my playful smile, the green smoke slithering over my limbs morphed into thick, healthy cornstalks. I hummed and swayed, letting the stalks curl around my breasts; cupping my chest like cats' tails, they wound over my bronzed flesh to form a living, verdant dress. As I pumped my hips, a lean glint of thigh gleamed through the stalks of my fringed skirt.

I sang in a husky siren's voice, "What do you want, Earl?" *I want to kill you.*

"I want you to kiss me." He gasped, the air snatched from his throat, his skin feverish with lust. He lost himself in me. I knew he felt my life force, a strong drum beat in the center of his gut. He licked his lips, his mouth dry, and I, so lush and green and fecund before him. He yearned to drink from my fountain.

"Close your eyes, Earl." I paused, studying the tiny blue veins in his fluttering eyelids, and grinned. The warm earthiness of my voice enveloped his ears. "Open your mouth, Earl." *Open your mouth so I can kill you.*

Earl opened his mouth to receive my communion, lulled by the pulsing symphony surrounding him. He waited. I lifted my arms. My palms turned upwards, as two javelins of green stalks shot from my wrists, piercing Earl's bony shoulders. Red jellyfish billowed on the waves of his white shirt. Stalks burrowed through his collarbone, prying, eager for purchase on the wall behind him. Tiles shattered around his head. Sharp bits grazed his cheek, and a trickle of blood ran down his skin. Earl's eyes bulged and he gasped, sobbing, sinking in fear and hot pain. I felt pleasure for the first time in months.

"Kiss me now," I commanded. *Kiss me now so I can finish you, Earl.*

An army of stalks snaked over my wrists, as bloody tears ran down his cheeks. The stalks drilled through the stringy gristle of his Achilles tendons. Searing ruby waves of torment lapped at his toes. He cried out, but I showed him no mercy, as he'd given none to his victims. He was nothing more than a wad of spit on the pavement.

"Sssh." I pressed a cool green stalk to his trembling mouth and peeled it away with vicious glee, slicing his lower lip, jeering at him as his eyes rolled back in his head, showing the whites. Blood ran down his chin. *That one was for Mom.*

"Please, no!"

"*Tsk-tsk-tsk.* Do you really think I'm going to let you go, Earl? After what you've done?"

I rubbed my nose against his clammy cheek. Earl opened his mouth to scream as a green stalk slithered down his throat, smothering his pleas. I grasped the four stalks pinning Earl to the wall like a quivering insect and pulled myself closer to him, using their thick, green serpentine flesh as ropes until my thighs pressed against his. My green dress skittered over his skin, cocooning him in stalks and leaving only his face free, my breath sweet on his lips.

"I've shown you so much, Earl, so much more than those other girls have shown you. Haven't I?" I leered at him, my teeth blazing white in the semi-darkness. He saw the dead girls reflected in my eyes, sprawled like broken ragdolls in fields of green. I loomed closer and closer. He shut his eyes tight, struggling to break free.

"Kiss me, Earl. Kiss me, so I can kill you." A glistening ear of yellow corn slid from my lips. With a wet *squish-crunch,* it punched through the shredded meat of his tongue, burying itself in the tiles behind him. Earl's body slumped against the broken wall.

It was done. In whispers of dried flesh, the corn stalks unfurled themselves from my body, fading into wispy green entrails and dissolving into nothing as I retrieved my top from the bathroom floor. I shook loose the dust of the broken yellow tiles and put it on, walking over to the sink to rinse out my mouth, admiring my handiwork and checking underneath my red nails for blood, grinning.

MY LITTLE RED WAGON

June 2002

It smelled like cinnamon, spicy and overpowering and sat cross-legged in Bobbie Mae's wagon beside her bed. The ceiling fan whirred, and the girl thing opened its mouth and began to chant in an eerie, rhythmic, sing-song voice, "You can't ride in my little red wagon. The front wheel's broken and the axle's draggin'. You can't ride in my little red wagon. Any. More. Today." It leered at Bobbie Mae, showing two sharp rows of shark teeth glowing against its banshee skin the blue-white color of milk, its long dark hair twisting serpentine in the gentle breeze from the fan. It loomed closer, its haunted eyes searching and hungry as its sing-song voice rose in the night. "Second verse. Same as the first. A little bit louder and a whole lot worse." It grinned, placing one bare foot onto the carpet. Its cold toes sinking into the plush pile, it swayed as it chanted. "You can't ride my little red wagon. The front wheel's broken and the axle's draggin'. You can't ride in my little red wagon. Any. More. Today."

Bobbi Mae bit down on the inside of her cheek, tasting the salt of her blood as she scrunched her nose to keep from crying. "Go away." She whimpered, her sweaty fists crumpling her sheet.

It placed its other bare foot on the carpet, leering over Bobbi Mae's face, so close, Bobbi Mae saw no reflection of her frightened face in its empty eyes. She felt a hot stream run down her leg and seep into the sheets.

"Third verse! Same as the second! A whole lot louder and a whole lot worse!"

"No!" Bobbi Mae struggled to free her trapped toes from the bedsheet.

"You can't ride my little red wagon! The front wheel's broken and the axle's draggin'!" Bobbi Mae grabbed Mr. Bear and dashed from her room, a burst of adrenaline rushing through her veins like heat lightning and behind her, Bobbi Mae heard the soft *shoosh-shoosh* of its dress as it padded toward the bedroom door.

***

May 2003

Dallas loved the third floor of his new house. He imagined pirates, ghosts, bats, and all sorts of cool stuff once roamed up here in the ancient musty smell; even an escaped convict kept secretly by his family while they worked hard to clear his name. The attic was boiling and stuffy, but still neat. The ceiling sloped low on the east side of the house with a view of the yard—a couple of acres of boyhood freedom to run, play baseball, and build a tree house or two. The best summer ever!

A fair-sized object stood covered with a green tarp in the far corner of the attic. Dallas sneezed, kicking up a thick layer of dust with his chucks. He would lug his mother's vacuum upstairs later and clean before he moved his boxes and his bed. Grinning, he thought about painting the walls black and putting up a model of the working solar system in glow-in-the-dark stickers or black light art, if his mom would let him.

A mummified pigeon lay before the hidden treasure as Dallas whisked the tarp away with a grand flourish. *Only a Radio Flyer wagon.* Not for babies, but not for boys his age, either. His smile widened anyway as he thought up uses for it; towing rocks back and forth to build a dam on the stream running across the property would be cool, and it was a free wagon. Mom always said free things were good.

"Junior?" His dad poked his tall, awkward frame up from the stairway, crouching in the low doorway. "You need some help with things?" He sniffed, rubbing his face, the broken blood vessels in his nose standing out against a fresh sunburn. "Looks like you need to vacuum, kiddo." He surveyed the attic. "Pretty hot up here. We can talk your Mom into buying a few fans. Dinner's in five minutes; we're having beans and hot dogs." His dad winked and turned, ducking to avoid bumping his head on the low ceiling on his way downstairs.

"Thanks, Dad!"

His mom came trudging up the stairs, dragging the ancient relic of a vacuum behind her. "Your father said you needed this. Hurry downstairs, okay?"

"'Kay."

***

Half an hour after dinner, his dad knelt, sweating like a racehorse, putting his bedframe together. Dallas inventoried his boxes of books and decided to put his desk under the window where it was nice and bright. His bed faced east with a view of the orchard. *This was going to be sweet.* Dallas grunted, his hands all smudged and grungy, a smear of grime striped across his cheek as he shoved one bookcase into the corner as far to the sloping wall as he could. He wanted them on either side of the desk to reference while he worked on his models.

He grabbed the red wagon by the handle, relishing the cool feel of the metal, hoping his mother would come back from the store with those fans soon, before he melted faster than Elvis in Madame Tussaud's. He steered the wagon out of the path of the other bookcase. The wheels squeaked a little from neglect, but he could fix them. With a weary sigh, Dallas mustered up the energy to push the other bookcase beside the desk. There—finished. Now he could unpack his books.

A yellowed newspaper poked out from the rafters, folded in fours. Dallas tugged hard. Too dark in the attic to read without his lamps, he scrambled to the window and sat down at his desk, spreading the newspaper out before him.

A picture of a young girl smiled up at him, her bangs cut blunt across her face, her long hair tied in a side ponytail with a silky pink ribbon. She wore a blue and pink checked dress like something Dallas's younger cousin Josie would wear and her brown eyes were huge and mischievous. Dallas smiled as he turned his attention to the article. The smile promptly slipped from his lips as he read: Gina Johnson was hit by a car on Thursday afternoon while playing with her brother, Thomas. The driver had no time to stop as the little girl rushed into the street after her runaway wagon. She received the Radio Flyer wagon for her sixth birthday earlier that summer. It was her favorite toy.

Dallas swore he felt the steely intensity of someone's eyes on his shoulders, but when he turned around, only the red Radio Flyer sat silent in the middle of the room, his throat tighter than Houdini's straitjacket, the air hot and dry in his lungs. He put down the newspaper and the chair scraped the worn wooden floorboards with a *screech!* as he rose from the desk. It was only a child's wagon, and yet, tiny droplets of sweat slid down the small of his back. Dallas tried to sing away his fear. "I've got a really cool car. All the girls want to kiss me," he sang in a quavering, preadolescent voice, his eyes glued to the wagon as he took one step and then another, coming closer and closer. A warm breeze from the window behind him rustled the paper and he jumped, nerves suddenly on fire. "All the girls want to ride with me," he sang, his voice cracking at the end of the line as he knelt, his hand on the wagon. The wagon seemed to zing with life as he stroked its red painted surface. He grabbed it by the handle with one hand and grabbed the back end with the other to turn it over, laying the wagon on its side. He sang in a whisper, "We're going to drag race down by the ri—" the line ending as he saw the initials scratched into the bottom of the wagon bed. *G.J.*

No, it couldn't be. His mind scrambled, trying to fathom the *exact* coincidence of finding a wagon with the very same initials of the dead girl in the newspaper, in the attic of his new house. He belted out to chase away the terrors, "You say you wanna go for a ride. Baby, I'll let you in. I might just give you a run for your money…" His voice trailed off as the breeze rustled the newspaper on the desk again.

Rising with slow deliberateness, Dallas headed for the stairway, just to see what his parents were up doing. *Just to see*, he thought. Not because he was afraid. He wasn't a baby. He was ten years old. Ghost stories were for babies. It was just a wagon. And yet, he walked backward to the stairs, never taking his eyes from the cheery red Radio Flyer in the middle of the room.

***

The new sounds of the house settling underneath him would take some getting used to; but Dallas pushed his uneasiness down and stretched out in bed, knowing his parents were just down the hall. He watched the trees catch the moon in the wind, listening to the hooting of the barn owls and the crickets chirping. Lightning bugs romped in the shadows beneath the orchard, tiny pinpoints of yellow-white light. The fans whirred, stirring the hot smell of cardboard boxes and dust around him. It would air out in a day or two and he had most of his boxes unpacked. His mind wandered. Tomorrow morning, he would hang his model airplanes above his desk and ask his dad to take him to the hardware store for paint for his walls. As he drifted off to sleep, one eye focused on the wagon before his lids slipped shut. He wasn't afraid of a little girl's wagon. He wasn't afraid at all.

***

Something shifted on the floorboards by the stairway. Dallas lay still, breathing shallowly so it couldn't see the rise and fall of his chest. He bit down on his knuckles, wishing he had a blanket between him and the dark night—something more substantial than just the sheet he'd thrown on the bed, but it'd been sweltering before. His parents promised to put in a window AC unit that weekend. *His parents.*

Dallas chanced a glance at the stairway—a huddled form sat in the wagon, swaying back and forth, blocking his only exit from the room. Why had he left the damn thing there? Now he had no escape. Dallas reached for his glasses on the stack of milk cartons he used for a nightstand. His fingers shook so he could hardly put them on his face. He swallowed a mouthful of spit as he watched the figure unfold, swinging its legs over the wagon bed. A small girl chanted, "You can't ride in my little red wagon. The front wheel's broken and the axle's draggin'. You can't ride in my little red wagon. Any. More. Today."

Dallas squeezed his eyes shut and gripped the sheet between his fingers with a feral ferocity. He struggled to hold back his stomach as a strong wave of cinnamon assaulted his nose and he tasted bile, his nose burning. Dallas sang softly, "You say you wanna go for a ride. Baby, I'll let you in. I might just give you a run for your money…"

The thing in the wagon sneered, pulling back its blackened lips to reveal white teeth, shaking its snarled mane of hair and singing louder over Dallas, "Second verse. Same as the first…"

Dallas continued singing, almost shouting now, "I've got a really cool car. All the girls want to kiss me…"

And still, the thing from the wagon sang, "You can't ride in my little red wagon. Any. More. Today. Third verse! Same as the second…"

While she continued to chant, Dallas belted out "Kiss…" His voice faded, and the air hung still. He opened one eye, expecting to see it hunched over in the wagon, long hair streaming over its face, showing a mere glimpse of its hungry, haggard eyes.

But the wagon rested—empty. Dallas rolled over on his side, away from the wagon. He was not a baby. He was not afraid of a silly old wagon.

The next morning, he carried the wagon downstairs and out through the kitchen door to the backyard.

"Where are you going with that thing?" His dad looked up from his morning bowl of cornflakes and the newspaper.

"Out to the shed."

"I thought you were going to keep it." His mom sipped her cup of chamomile tea.

"Nah, wagons are for babies. I'm going to store it in the shed."

"Alright." She shrugged and reached for the Sports section of the newspaper with one hand while blindly reaching for a slice of buttered toast with the other.

"Dad, can we take it to the landfill this weekend? It gives me the creeps."

"Don't you want some other little kid to enjoy it?"

"No, it's haunted."

CARNIVOROUS COWS FROM OUTER SPACE

I've been told by my superiors I sound like the bipeds Ron Perlman and James Earl Jones if they were both chain smokers hopped up on horse steroids and drank like fish, though I never made the acquaintance of a drunken fish. Anyway, that's not relevant to the story. What is relevant to the story and, really all you need to know, is that my name is Mooligan, not to be confused with the word "hooligan," though I can understand the confusion, since they are so close in print. My human captors (or so they think) call me "Cow 152," but I assure you my I.Q. is much higher than 152 and I have never needed a "do-over" for anything in my 205 years of existence, though if I end up at the stockyard any time soon, I might need to contact you from the other side of the pasture. Nevertheless, I am attempting to befriend *Homo sapiens* and reach a peaceable existence as Planet Moo is doomed for demolition in the year 2008. You bipeds may laugh lightly at Douglas Adams' *The Hitchhiker's Guide to the Galaxy*, but I assure you it holds some truth. You may also think we are only cows, but really, we are intelligent quadrupeds from Planet Moo. (Moo translates into "Superior Beings" in our native language of Moolian, but to you human bipeds, it sounds like "steak.")

This is precisely why my species is miffed these days. In trying to save our species from annihilation, we managed to become food for lower less intelligent lifeforms like you—except for those nice East Indian folks. Being Hindu, they believe we have souls. Plus, they rely on us for dairy products and use our waste as a source of fuel and fertilizer. We are a revered matriarchal symbol. Hence, it is safe to be a cow in India, minus a few slaughterhouses they're trying to have unsuccessfully shut down and nowhere else is it safe, unless you live in a hippie commune. Though personally, after observing Hindus vs. hippie communes, I am more inclined to favor the former than the latter. One can only listen to Allen Ginsberg's *Howl* so many times and frankly, I never could stomach performance art. Nor do I understand the hippie infatuation with what you bipeds deem "grass." It has a most cantankerous flavor that is quite unpalatable, really. Frankly, I wouldn't feed it to a goat, and they aren't even as intelligent as me. (This I have witnessed many times at what you humans call "petting zoos" where many a young biped's paper nametag has fallen prey to a goat's insatiable appetite for junk.)

But I digress. All you need to know is that my name is Mooligan, I come from the Planet Moo, and I am trying to take over your world for Cowkind everywhere. (You may ask where Planet Moo is, and my response in simple layman's terms, to steal a line from your beloved biped George Lucas, is: In a galaxy far, far away. And that's all you need to know. It's top secret, so don't ask anymore, or I will have to do something drastic that you won't like.)

At this moment, my battle for cow sovereignty appears to be a losing one. (I am not prepared to admit Earthling bipeds might be smarter than us, but they certainly have proved detrimental to our existence. Perhaps it's our lack of opposable thumbs.) At this time, I am unsure why all my reinforcements keep ending up in the stockyards, and it seems industrialization is taking over my small corner of the pasture—quite literally. It is a small pasture in the middle of an industrial park in the suburbs of Dallas, Texas, steakhouse capital of the United States. And this morning, I witnessed a rotund tobacco-spitting biped hammering a post into the ground by my feeding trough. The post had a sign. The sign read: Land for Sale. My land for sale. My sweet green bliss of pasture sandwiched between a paper company and too many dot coms and financial institutions for me to count on my hooves. And much to my bovine chagrin, a new McDeath popped up across the street. All of this I will be reporting to my superiors in our weekly meetings, but in the meantime, I had plenty of hours to while away in pastoral bliss, or what was left of my pastoral bliss.

My pastoral bliss was being interrupted by a routine morning visit from a biped I fondly referred to as Joe Blackberry. Joe walked with a manly business swagger of importance with his Blackberry permanently attached to his hands like an extra appendage. He practically farted money, as his lavish label-oriented wardrobe indicated. This week he favored Versace and Nordstrom, and to my pleasant surprise, imported Italian leather that I did not recognize as my cousin Vinnie from my missions abroad. And he reeked of the funny-smelling water you bipeds call "cologne." He tended to favor horrendous odiferous scents like Burberry.

Joe Blackberry liked to talk loud enough to be heard above a sonic boom, which for non-science-oriented bipeds is typically around 167 megawatts per square meter and sometimes exceeds 200 decibels. (As a further reference point, thunder is a sonic boom that occurs naturally during a thunderstorm. Just to give you an idea of how loud Joe Blackberry can project on a sunny day in my quiet end of the pasture while stinking up the place with his Burberry cologne.)

Each morning at precisely nine o'clock, Joe Blackberry sneaked into my pasture to call the woman he cheated with on his wife. Joe Blackberry didn't want to be overheard moo-ning over a female biped who wasn't his mate by his office superiors as he coveted a cushy corner office with a leather chair imported from Italy and made from my other cousin, Veal. His carnal sin's name was Candi. Not very original, but he loved to call her lots of cutesy foo-foo names like "pumpkin" and "doll face" that would make any grown bull cringe, what you bipeds like to call "pet names." Though if I had a pet, I'd name it something cool like George W. Bush or Dick Cheney. Then I could call out for my pet in the pasture: Here Georgie, Georgie! C'mere, boy! And he'd come bounding over with love and adoration in his *Homo sapien* eyes. But I digress again…

This morning Joe Blackberry was discussing the ways he would love to, as he put it so romantically, "boink" Candi. If I didn't have four stomachs, I would have suffered from the ultimate gag reflex. Joe Blackberry's whiny castrato voice carried over the mild morning breeze, mingling with the greasy fast-food scent of McDeath from across the street, and as I watched the lights flicker in the sign on top of the fast food joint, I imagined I heard thousands of my comrades mooing in distress.

Depressed, I turned my attention back to Joe Blackberry, instantly cheered by Joe's debacle. Joe Blackberry had stepped in a pile of cow shit. "What the fuck! Stupid fuckin' cow shit! Hold on a second, Candi."

Amused, I looked up from my morning trough, along with my comrades, to find Joe Blackberry scraping the bottom of his alligator loafer on the edge of my breakfast plate.

"What are you looking at?"

I mooed a reply, to which Joe Blackberry shot back, "Stupid cow. Should make a fuckin' burger outta you an' show you who's boss. Bet you'd taste good with some A-1."

At which point a great anger swelled within my broad muscled chest, and while Joe Blackberry was busy wiping the bottom of his shoe with a McDeath napkin from across the street that he conveniently had tucked in his pocket after breakfast this morning, I sauntered casually around my breakfast trough and headbutted him to the ground, relishing the look of fear in his beady piggy eyes. (No offense to you pigs, though. But he did have piggy eyes. I have nothing but the highest regard for intelligent life forms from other planets and I've read *Charlotte's Web* more than a few times with a teary eye on longer intergalactic vacations with my youngest calf, Angus.)

Joe Blackberry caterwauled like a terrified coyote, and I saw my snorting nostrils reflected in the shiny wet pupils of his eyes as I held him down with my hooves, breathing hot on his neck. I licked the salty sweat from his brow and then sank my teeth into his jugular. In between hot, fresh mouthfuls of *Homo sapiens*, I remarked to the other cows in the pasture, "Huh, they taste like chicken." Score one for the away team. This cow wasn't taking any bull from anybody anymore, anytime, anywhere. I'd taken matters into my own hooves, and I liked it. In fact, the only thing missing from my after-breakfast snack was some mayo and ketchup and that yummy shredded lettuce they use at McDeath. Of course, a full report would be expected on my superior's desk by morning, which is standard policy in the involvement of any *Homo sapiens* death, since I was supposed to be a peaceful ambassador to humankind. But I was confident my superiors would approve of my actions, and if not, too bad for Joe Blackberry. There were plenty more where he came from.

"Anybody got a toothpick? I've got something stuck in my bottom left molar." At this point, I remembered the debacle of not having hands. *Oh wait. I don't have opposable thumbs or my beloved pet monkey, Chips, with me. Damn.* Guess I was spending the morning with the remains of Joe Blackberry between my teeth, but my eyes gleamed with glee as I saw an empty alligator loafer lying beside my trough. Never again would my breakfast be interrupted with the coital fantasies of a horny *Homo sapiens* teenager trapped in the overactive imagination of a thirty-something professional. Sadly, as I was walking away, I recognized the alligator shoe as my good friend from Paris, La Coste.

***

At this point, I caught Moorice staring at a new visitor approaching our corner of the pasture. (For you lesser intelligent beings, Moorice is pronounced "Moo-reese," not "Moo-rice", as in the Asian dish. Moorice is one of my newer recruits, though he is working out quite nicely now that he's mastered the art of silence when following orders. He tended to be a bit chatty before.) "Boss, I think we have visitors."

"Your deduction skills astound me sometimes, Moorice."

"What?"

"Hmmm… Nothing, nothing," I barked. (Though not really. I mean, you wouldn't think a cow would bark like a canine, would you? You can't be that daft.) "Move your hooves so I can get a better look at him." I craned my neck in their general direction, pretending to munch lazily on my leftover breakfast.

"But this is pri-iiime real estate you have here, Mr. Raaa-mesh." The big lug of a Texan in his Armani suit adjusted his belt, which I noted was made from one of my former superiors, Elsie the Borden mascot, instantly sealing the poor unsuspecting twit's fate on my assignment.

I whispered to Moorice, "You take the stumpy one that smells like bacon with the bad B.O. I'll take the other one." What Andy Armani, as I fondly remember him, and Ramesh heard, though, was: Moooo! Moo! Moo! (At this point I would like to take the time to educate you, the reader, about our native dialect of "Moolian." Much like some northern bipeds, Eskimos for example, have a polysynthetic language resulting in derivational suffixes and noun-incorporation to describe subtle nuances where a single word can mean an entire phrase, the same is true for our native language. This is why all a *Homo sapiens* will hear is the word "moo." But really, we're carrying on an intelligent conversation. Who woulda thunk it?)

"Well, what's got his tail in a knot this morning? Cute big feller, ain't he? Too bad he'll be on his way to the stockyards soon with the new development."

"Mr. Kensington, I cannot purchase this land from you."

"Well, tie me 'roun an armadillo an' throw me inna Trinity River. Why on God's green acres not?"

"Because of the cows, Mr. Kensington. My family is Hindu, though I am an atheist myself, but if my grandmother in India ever found out about this, she would be very displeased with me. And that's putting it mildly. I greatly respect my grandmother and want to live to see my thirtieth birthday."

"You can't buy the land because of the cows?"

My ears perked up and I regarded Ramesh with a strong reverence I reserved only for my highest superiors and my wife and children back home. Perhaps not all *Homo sapiens* deserved to be food after all.

"No, I cannot. You see, where I come from cows are sacred because of their life-giving milk. My grandmother would weep if I sent a whole herd of such beautiful animals to the slaughter yards. I'm sorry, but I cannot buy this land from you." Ramesh walked away, bowing his head to me as he left the pasture. And I was kind of sorry to see the cute little fella go. He would have made a good ally. Perhaps I was going to have to research the Hindu community in and around Dallas further for my superiors' weekly report. If their numbers were strong, they might be able to aid our cause.

However, Mr. Kensington fell into the F.O.O.D category. I nudged Moorice with my nose. "You take the left and I'll take the right. The rest of you bring up the rear." I nodded to the herd behind me.

Ironically, Mr. Kensington tripped over Joe Blackberry's lone alligator loafer by the side of my trough as he was exiting the pasture. At the exact moment he tripped, his cell phone rang. My mild Dallas morning was interrupted by a tinny Michael Jackson belting *Thriller* from Mr. Kensington's phone.

Perhaps a small primordial part of Mr. Kensington's ill-used brain sparked alive, a prehistoric caveman snippet of him that remembered a time when he was prey on the menu and still fairly young on the food chain. Or perhaps, it was the loud belch I let out when Joe Blackberry started to not agree with my four stomachs, but Mr. Kensington turned around right then. He resembled Skippy when he was surprised, the fantail goldfish I used to have back on Planet Moo as a young calf, all pop-eyed and round-mouthed. Or maybe he looked like someone slammed his tongue in a pickup door. (I once knew a young calf that happened to in an unfortunate farm accident. He couldn't talk properly for the rest of his career. And every time he opened his mouth, all we heard was "Mmmth!" And so he became useless to our cause in the field, and was put on permanent filing duty at The Division of Moo-tor Vehicles in Plano. Which is hard to do without opposable thumbs, but he had a pet monkey too, so it worked out all right. Well, for him, not the monkey. The monkey was bored, but I digress again…)

So anyway, Mr. Kensington turned around at that exact moment all fishy bug-eyed, and saw about twenty pairs of brown steer eyes staring back at him with ravenous intent. (If this scene had been animated, instead of dollar signs reflected in our eyes, I like to imagine we'd have had Steak N' Shake neon signs reflected in ours.) Mr. Kensington made a valiant attempt at scaling the pasture fence, but as he was losing the battle with his waistline and had spent one too many mornings at McDeath across the street eating sausage McDeaths, he wasn't spry enough to pull his pudge over the fence—so sad for him, but good for us. Another enemy fell behind our lines, though he would have tasted better with some fava beans and a nice Chianti. (Well, not literally. You don't really think I have a kitchen and wine fridge just sitting around the old pasture, do you now? I mean, I am an intelligent life form capable of intergalactic travel with the flick of a tail, but that's going a bit far even for you, reader.)

Moochelle took this moment to show up from her constant preening. (She thinks her tail is better than the rest of us, but her farts are just as smelly, trust me. You don't want to be on the tail end of that heifer). "Where'd the stumpy bald guy go?"

"He had a late breakfast engagement." I grinned, hoping I didn't have any Kensington stuck in my bottom molars.

She rolled her eyes and flicked a fly off her round rump with her tail. "Oh, I rather liked him. What's for breakfast?"

"Don't you mean lunch? It's almost lunch time. Really, if you showed up for our morning meetings and kept to a regular schedule, Moochelle, you'd be more of an asset than an ass. We need to figure out how to save our pasture and stop feeding the stockyards, or we'll never be able to save our species from imminent destruction."

She huffed and blew her hairy lips at me in a wet raspberry, but soon lost interest as she saw a young leggy blonde waving a Chick-fil-A sandwich as she straddled the pasture fence in her black Versace Trapunto boots. She resembled a flamingo on stilts with her hot pink Burberry trench, which she obviously wore for fashion reasons only, as the day was warming up to be hotter than a cow pie. Bulimic Betsy, as I named her a few weeks ago, had a secret to keep from her coworkers. And the pasture was the only deserted place in the industrial park, or so she thought. She quickly gobbled down her Chick-fil-A sandwich. (Chick-fil-A is one of my most successful campaign projects to date, and chickens aren't known to be intelligent creatures, so there's no loss of allies there. They eat rocks. How bright is that? My superiors were quite pleased with the slogan: Eat More Chicken. Sadly, McDeaths were still popping up faster than flies.) "Shoulda had a burger," she mumbled with her mouth full.

"Your table awaits, madam." I nodded at our unsuspecting dinner entrée. It's a good thing I'd been assigned to a fairly busy pasture, or we would have all starved and never completed any further assignments. My superiors might not like my decision to eat them instead of befriending them, but the latest stockyard statistics were sure to change their minds.

Did you know reader that cows can eat up to eight hours a day? Why, if every cow ate one *Homo sapiens* per hour per day of their normal eating schedule, the world would be a better, more peaceful place. Don't you think? I think so. Now if you'll excuse me, I have another meal to attend.

WHAT HAPPENED IN THE COUNTRY

"You'll have to excuse the mess. I'm still unpacking. You know how it is the first week you move in," Kathryn said as they walked back to the house. She made a mental note to call the painters her friend Irene recommended, scowling at the peeling paint on the shutters and gingerbread trim. She silently thanked Irene for also recommending the contractor who inspected the house before she signed the lease. At least she knew the wood wasn't rotting.

The kitchen was a bright daffodil yellow and quite spacious, overlooking the backyard. Kathryn opened a cupboard. "Oh dear, I've only unpacked one mug, it seems. Let me find another," she said, burying her copper curls in a large cardboard box. "I've only unpacked one of everything so far," her voice came muffled. "You know how it is when you live alone." A triumphant smile on her face, Kathryn emerged with a white cup in hand, her red bandana slipping to her neck.

Sylvia paused, unsure what to say, fingering the tinfoil covering her plate of sugar cookies.

"You were hoping that a nice young couple was moving in here, right?"

"Oh, no." Sylvia shook her head as an uncertain smile graced her lips. "It's just, being so far out of town, well, it would have been nice to have a young, strong man around here." It would be nice to continue the tradition of the Green Man Sect with someone, but it looked like that wasn't going to happen. She could scare Kathryn away like she'd scared other people away that just didn't seem like the right fit for the land.

"Would you like some tea?"

"Yes, please. It will go nicely with the sugar cookies I made you."

"Oh, thank you. You're such a dear. You live alone too?" Kathryn put the teapot on to boil.

"Yes, yes, I do. My Henry passed on about eight years ago, and since then, it's just been me in that big house."

"In the yellow house next door?" She smiled to herself, thinking about how far away "next door" was, really—more than three city blocks. Plenty of room between her and her neighbor to do as she pleased. Why, she could even put a pool in the backyard and go skinny dipping and no one would bother her.

"No. I'm on the corner, the white house with the red trim."

"Oh, next to the McKinleys. I met them yesterday. Nice people. They gave me the name of a tree trimmer."

Sylvia's bluebird eyes widened. "Oh, really? What tree are you having trimmed?"

The shrill whistle of the teapot interrupted their conversation.

Why does she care so much about a tree? Kathryn wondered. *Perhaps she was one of those old ladies who couldn't bear to kill even one dandelion. My Nanny was like that.* She smiled, getting out two bags of mint tea and setting them in the cups to steep. She carried them over to the table by the picture window overlooking the backyard. *What a mess those trees are.* She didn't want to worry about raking all those leaves come fall. "I'm having some of the oaks cut down."

"Really?"

Kathryn watched an icy anger freeze over Sylvia's blue eyes. *Great, I've made enemies with Granny Tree Hugger.* She occupied herself with dunking her tea bag repeatedly in her cup, letting the sweet scent of mint soothe her like a balm. "Yes. The house is so isolated during the daytime, so dark with all these trees. I thought I'd have the ones closest to the house cut down, and the rest thinned out."

"Oh, dear."

"You seem upset, Sylvia. I didn't mean to upset you."

Sylvia blinked, staring into her tea. "It's just that these trees have been here since I was a child."

"Did you come here often as a child?"

"Oh, yes, I was friends with their daughter, Margaret."

"Whose daughter?"

"Why, the MacArds. They were the only people who ever lived in the place for any length of time—until you came, of course. I'm sure you'll be here awhile." Sylvia lifted her cup to her lips. *Not if I can help it.*

"Well, what happened to them?"

"The MacArds always lived here, until Mr. MacArd moved away when his wife passed on. Margaret would have lived here by herself, if she had lived."

"What happened to her?" Kathryn's heartbeat filled her ears and the oaks outside leaned closer to the house, listening. It could have been her imagination, but she thought she saw their black gnarled branches swaying, though the windmill outside by the garden shed at the back of the property did not turn. *Strange.* A chill crept into her throat, not even chased away by the tea she gulped, hardly tasting it.

"There was a terrible accident. One summer Margaret and her brothers were out playing at one of the abandoned farms when she fell into a covered well. The board was wet and rotten, and she went right through. Her brother, Tad, went for help, but by the time his father and older brother came, she'd drowned, passed out from a concussion in three feet of water."

"That's horrible."

"You know the stand of lilac bushes about five miles up the road?"

"Yes," Kathryn nodded. She remembered them well because when she moved in, she planned to go back and pick some for her bedroom. Lilacs were her favorite.

"Her daddy, Collin, planted those as a memorial. The farm's burned down now, caught fire in a lightning storm about four years back, but those lilacs are still standing." She sipped her tea, smiling with her yellowed teeth at Kathryn.

"That's a sad story."

"You live long enough, and you will see some sad things." Sylvia gazed out the window at the oaks.

Kathryn, aware of Sylvia's thoughts, rushed to speak, "Well, I can assure you, Sylvia, that I won't cut down all the trees, just the ones closest to the house and any that are sick."

"But not that large one before the raspberry bushes. It's the oldest one."

"And the prettiest." Kathryn smiled. "No, I won't be cutting that great one down, but I will be glad to get rid of the ones closer to the house. They're not good for my roof, and those squirrels scampering around out there give me the willies. I think there might even be one trapped in my attic." She shuddered.

"Yes, those squirrels can be bothersome, and so can old ladies who take up too much of your time." She rose, smoothing the front of her housedress as she set down her cup of tea.

"Oh, no. You're not bothering me, really." Relieved the woman wanted to leave Kathryn to her gardening, Kathryn stood up, adjusting her bandana. The break from the monotony of the overgrown raspberry patch had been pleasant, but she needed to get back to work. She wanted to finish by dinnertime.

"It was very nice to meet you, Kathryn."

"Yes, I had a pleasant visit," Kathryn said, repressing the urge to scratch the hairs rising on the back of her neck as she thought of Margaret. *Yes, it's always nice to meet new neighbors over a nice cup of death.* "Well, don't be a stranger now. You come back any time." *But don't. There's something off about you.*

"I'll do that. Enjoy your cookies."

Kathryn was reminded of how yellow Sylvia's teeth were as her thin, pale lips stretched into a smile. "Thank you very much. I'll return the plate as soon as I'm finished."

"No hurry." Sylvia paused on the last step.

***

Kathryn worked right through lunch until dinner, her aching shoulders, blistered feet, and bramble-scratched arms begging for a hot bath. Exhausted, she trudged upstairs, shedding her clothes on the steps as she went. There was no one to argue with about it. She lived alone and she could damn well do as she pleased. Why, she could even cook, vacuum, and scrub the kitchen floor naked if she wanted. She felt young, spunky, and rebellious. *Perhaps I'll hire a maid who could cook and clean for me*, she thought, *so I can go out and play and buy a new car and find some hot young piece of twenty-one-year-old manhood to toss around the bedroom. No reason Steve should have all the fun. The dirty rotten snake. Why had he left her, anyway?*

She examined her body before the full-length mirror in the white bathroom. She still had a nice firm figure. She smoothed her palm over her stomach, turning sideways, her blistered feet screaming for attention. She winced. Thankfully, she had unpacked at least this room. Kathryn searched the linen closet, forgetting where she put her bath salts. Her hand brushed against something cold and leathery at the back of the shelf.

She pulled out a book, an ancient book, its green leather spine mottled and cracked. As she blew a thick layer of dust from the cover, she wrinkled her nose at the smell of dampness and mothballs, opening it. She didn't remember it being there before. Outside the trees pressed closer to the house, their limbs blackened in the light of dusk. Curious, she decided to read it before bed. Right now, she wanted a good hot bath and some supper. The book could wait.

Kathryn located a packet of lavender bath salts and sat down on the edge of the deep, cast-iron tub with clawed feet, just like Nanny's. Smiling, she drew the hot water, pouring the bath salts into the steaming tub, her shoulders relaxing as the salts hissed and bubbled a bit, giving the water a slight purple tinge, the air pregnant with the clean, sharp scent of lavender. Turning off the faucet, she sank into her little piece of bliss, relishing the stillness of the house and the hot water over her toes. The previous owner left the bathroom tiled completely in white—a little stark for her taste. Kathryn made a mental note to go shopping for curtains when she had the time. She sighed, scrubbing her back with a loofah. This house was so old and there was so much to do, the trees, removing the raspberry patch, putting in the koi pond, the patio, and the gazebo, finalizing her divorce. She scrubbed faster as she thought about Steve, trying to wash away the dirty memory of her marriage.

Refreshed and aching from the day's work, Kathryn emerged from the tub and wrapped up in a plush white robe. She grabbed the mysterious book from her bedroom and ventured downstairs to the kitchen to make a fresh pesto sauce and pasta. She even added extra garlic just because Steve detested it, an imp's grin igniting her green eyes. Somewhere, she knew she had a bottle of Merlot they'd been saving for their anniversary this year. "Ha!" Her laughter punched the silence. Kathryn commenced on a mad pillage of the boxes spilling from the kitchen into the formal dining room, emerging triumphant with a bottle in hand. "Eat my tight ass, Steve-O," she cried as she popped the cork.

Exuberant and starving, she did not bother to locate a wine glass. Carrying her plateful of steaming pasta and the opened bottle, and with the book tucked into the pocket of her robe, she followed her trail of dirty clothes upstairs to the bedroom, kicking them out of the way with a well-manicured foot as she climbed the steps. She flipped the light switch with her elbow, casting a rosy glow from the wall sconces on either side of the bed, and sank into the middle of the down comforter, her plate resting on her crossed legs and the bottle of wine hugged firmly between her thighs. She fumbled underneath the comforter for the remote to the stereo and, finding it, pressed the power button. The angelic voice of Enya filled the room.

With a naughty snicker, Kathryn scooted back on the bed. Propping herself up with her pillows against the black headboard, she reveled in her wild abandon as she ate a forkful of pasta. Steve always hated her eating in the bedroom. She took a swig of Merlot. "Perfection," she whispered to the empty room. "Food, drink, and no man to ruin the atmosphere." She nestled into the covers as she finished eating, setting the empty plate beside the bed on the floor, but not the side she slept on. She didn't want to put a foot in cold, slimy pesto sauce on the way to the bathroom.

Still cradling the Merlot between her legs, she reached for the book she'd set on the nightstand. It felt gritty and worn like archaic earth beneath her fingertips. On the stereo, Enya finished playing and the CD changer switched to Paul Simon singing *Fifty Ways to Leave Your Lover.* Gritting her teeth, Kathryn advanced to the next song, her index finger punching the button on the remote. Paul Simon sang *Bridge Over Troubled Water.*

"I'll give you a bridge, Steve, a high one you can jump off," Kathryn growled, punching the forward button to advance to the next CD. Nancy Sinatra sang *These Boots Were Made for Walking.* With a serendipitous smile and a long celebratory swallow of Merlot, Kathryn returned to the book. The pages smelled musty as she flipped through the ghastly pictures of horned men with wild lust in their eyes pursuing frightened fawns, and men sneering with ferocious eyes, their faces shrouded by leaves. And one that chilled the wine slipping down her warm throat: a group of villagers wearing wreaths surrounding an altar, a kneeling man's face wrenched in agony as the leader stood above him, wielding a scythe. The accompanying text read: The May Day King was crowned and for the entirety of the growing season, given the honor of sleeping with a young maiden, the symbol of life and fertility, to ensure a bountiful crop for the village. However, at the end of the festival, he was sacrificed to The Green Man, so the God of the Forest would return next spring. Kathryn shuddered at the horrible image of the sacrifice. The room felt colder, and she rose to open the window to let in the warm night breeze, pausing to listen to the wind in the oaks. Their leaves whispered, "Give… Give," in a fleshy hushed chorus. She slammed the window shut, deciding to go to bed early. *Perhaps, it wasn't a good idea to drink tonight.* She would sleep it off and rise early tomorrow. There was a lot of work to be done, and the tree specialist was stopping by tomorrow morning. Slipping under the comforter and glad for the warmth, she set the alarm on the stereo and drifted off thinking about Nancy Sinatra's boots walking all over Steve. With a satisfied grin, she snuggled deeper into her pillow.

***

Kathryn awoke, naked, her bladder burning. Rain fell hard against the windows, bouncing off the rooftop. She frowned. She didn't remember the weatherman saying anything about rain. A clap of thunder rattled a loose shutter on the house and Kathryn jumped and stubbed her toe on her dresser beside the door. "Fuck, that hurts," she shouted to herself, limping to the bathroom. *I'll have to move the dresser just a tad to the right tomorrow.*

She did not need a flashlight as the lightning raged outside the bathroom, lighting it briefly in bursts of white. Rain sluiced down the window and the toilet seat was cold as she sat down to pee, cursing her injured, throbbing toe. Kathryn flushed and rooted around in the medicine cabinet above the sink for a bottle of Advil. Lightning struck outside again, and thunder pounded the sky with an angry fist.

Kathryn hobbled back to the comforting nest of her bed, grateful for the body heat still trapped between the covers as she slipped in, huddling down for warmth. Five minutes later and still awake, Kathryn threw back the covers, turning on the reading lamp beside her bed. Her gaze fell on the book and the smell of petrichor, which she loved, awakened her wild senses. Shivering and goosebumped, she hastily threw open her dresser drawers, looking for a pair of Steve's pajamas out of habit. "Oh, damn him to hell already, and his stupid pajamas too," she hissed through cold, clenched teeth, as she snatched her own plum thermal tee, yanking it over her head. Her hair was of deep flames; she stopped to look outside. Shadows of rain ran over her cheeks in the lightning's flash as she leaned closer to the darkness, her fingertips gripping the white ledge. *Someone's out there. There's someone in my backyard.* Ducking into the safety of the night beside the window, Kathryn peeked outside again. Another burst of lightning lit up the stand of oaks. *There.* Her breath was louder than the thunder in her ears. *A flap of white. Is it a nightgown?* Kathryn sucked in her breath, her stomach burning with acidic fear. *Boom!* A clap of thunder shook the shutters, and in the lightning's brief play, she saw it—a figure—a pale figure walking through the trees.

She drew back from the window, her fingertips pressed to her lips as she crept back to her bed, trying to make as little noise as possible, afraid the figure would see her.

"This is ridiculous, Kathryn," she told herself. "What are you afraid of? Just call the police." She pulled the covers up to her neck, comforted by the weight of the blankets pressing down on her. "And tell them what?" she asked out loud, her voice quivering. "That there's someone in my backyard in the middle of a storm? Damn it! Why do I not own a dog, something big and imposing with lots of teeth, sharp teeth, like a Doberman or a Rottweiler?" But she hated the smell of a wet dog and their slobbering doggy breath. "What am I afraid of?" she asked herself again in a hoarse whisper. Kathryn cast back the covers in a fit of protective rage, tromping to the window, barefoot. *Boom!* Another clap of thunder and another burst of lightning. She leaned over the windowsill, squinting.

The yard was empty.

"It must have been a trick of the storm. Silly woman," Kathryn scolded herself. "You see one little thing and you go running in fear."

She crawled back into bed. *But it's natural to be uneasy during a storm. It's a new house, a new yard. You just need to get used to it.* Rolling over on her side, she shut her eyes, harrumphing and rolling to the middle of the bed. *There is no "my side" anymore. The whole bloody thing is mine!* She opened her eyes. *But if there had been someone? No. It's probably a bag blowing in the storm, or a sheet that blew off someone's clothesline. It's windy out there, and I've been drinking. I'll see in the morning. Everything will be fine.*" And with a small sigh, she fell back asleep.

***

Morning came and with it the effervescent green after a good night's rain. While the tree removal guy inspected the property, Kathryn searched for signs of someone in her yard last night. She felt silly, really. No footprints sank into the ground beneath the oaks and the lock on the shed at the edge of the property wasn't broken. She did, however, find a plastic bag snagged in the raspberry patch. Chuckling to herself, she crumpled it in her hand, sucking on a wound where a bush pricked her finger.

"Ma'am?"

"Oh!" Kathryn jumped.

"I'm sorry. I didn't mean to startle you." The guy stood there in his blue jumpsuit, smiling.

His eyes are a nice shade of blue, almost a morning glory blue.

"Here's my quote." He ripped a pink sheet of paper from a clipboard with grimy fingernails. "If you'll just look it over and give me a call."

"No need," she said as she took it. "Just come back tomorrow morning. I want them gone—all of them. Except for the ones we talked about."

Her penetrating gaze made him squirm, and he wanted to run. "Yes, Ma'am." He stood, awkward and unsure whether to walk away.

"Well then," Kathryn chimed, a fake smile in her voice. "I'll see you tomorrow at nine o'clock." *Honestly, if the guy wasn't packing a set of beautiful pecs under that jumpsuit, he would be a walking waste of space.* She squinted at his nametag over his breast pocket. In red curlicue letters it read: Adam. "Thank you, Adam."

"Uh, Ma'am? One more thing. I found this nailed to one of the trees back here." He held up a patinaed coin the size of a silver dollar.

"What is that?" She snatched the coin from his hand, turning almost as green as the strange creature's face on its surface.

"Ma'am, are you alright?"

"I'm fine," she said.

"It's just a coin, ma'am." Adam studied Kathryn's haunted eyes.

"I know." She took a long, deep, breath, trying to still the feeling of moths fluttering in her throat, her knuckles white as she clasped it between her fingers. "If you'll excuse me, I have some work inside to do," she said, the words spilling from her mouth in a hurried jumble. "You know the way out."

"Yes, ma'am." Adam smiled at her, adjusting the brim of his blue cap, grinning like a winning racehorse at her back as she stalked toward the house, the coin clenched in her fist, her dark red hair bouncing in the dappled sunlight of the oaks.

Reeling with nausea, her stomach feeling twisted inside out and upside down, Kathryn threw the coin down on the kitchen counter. It wobbled three times on its edge before resting, silent. She spooked at the chime of the doorbell and ran to answer the door. "Karen."

"Hi, Kathryn." A tall blonde, holding a Boston fern.

"Come on in. The house's a mess, of course." She held the door open.

"Well, I just wanted to stop by to see how everything is going." She followed Kathryn into the kitchen, maneuvering through the maze of boxes.

"I can't tell you how nice it was to find a realtor to work with out here." Kathryn set a coffee mug on the counter. "Coffee?"

"Oh, no. I can't stay long. I have a showing in a little while, but I wanted to drop this off and congratulate you on your new home." She gestured to the fern on the counter. "How are you settling into Germantown? The neighbors treating you all right?"

"Oh, yes." Kathryn paused. "Well, there was this one tiny incident. Quite funny." Kathryn let out a forced laugh as she heated a mug of water in the microwave for coffee, which she'd unpacked earlier that morning, and filled her in.

"Oh?" Karen raised her thick eyebrows in question, her gaze landing on the green coin on the counter. The coin intrigued her. "May I have my son look at this coin? It could be worth something."

Kathryn returned to the breakfast bar, heaping spoonfuls of instant coffee into her mug. "Sure, I was going to show you that. It's dreadful, isn't it? The tree guy found it nailed to one of my oaks. The face on the coin is The Green Man, the protector of the forest. I read this awful book last night about sacrifices to him. I know this will sound silly, and it is." She laughed. "But I thought I saw someone in my backyard last night who put that coin there. It was stormy, but I couldn't shake the feeling someone was out there. And then, this morning I found this plastic bag in the raspberry patch, and I said to myself, 'There, Kathryn, there's your trespasser.' But I felt like I was being watched last night."

Karen placed a comforting hand over Kathryn's and said in her realtor's reassuring voice, "I'm sure it's nothing, really. The coin's probably been there for ages, and you just didn't know it. I heard tales of there being an old sect of people who worshipped The Green Man, but I never believed it until now. You found this coin and storms can freak out even the bravest of people, especially in a new house." She gestured to the boxes. "Well, I can see you're busy, so I'll just leave you to your unpacking." She stood to leave.

"Karen?"

Karen gave her an impatient smile, hoping Kathryn would let her go soon so she could make her appointment. "Yes?"

"You said this neighborhood is relatively crime free?"

"Of course it is. It's out in the country. What could possibly happen in the country?" Her words fell about one yard short of comforting.

Kathryn heard the eerie "Dueling Banjos" from *Deliverance* playing in her head. "Right. You're right. Let me walk you to the door. But that sect you were talking about? When did they stop gathering?"

"Oh, at least fifty years back, I would think." Karen fingered the green coin inside her pocket.

Kathryn watched Karen walk down the steps, marveling at how well Karen carried herself in stiletto pumps. *I should get some of those. They're sexy.* All worries about the coin and her late-night visitor were replaced by hot, racy thoughts of being single and out on the town for the night.

"By the way." Karen paused on the last step, grinning up at Kathryn. "Those geraniums look lovely."

"What? What geraniums?" Kathryn leaned out the door, a long, agile arm draped over the door frame, brushing her hair from her face as she stared at the Grecian planters, her heart settling like a gravestone in her stomach. "I—I didn't plant those."

Karen's grin grew wider, and she winked. "Sounds like someone already has a secret admirer," she sang in a schoolgirl's voice as she waltzed down the unpaved drive, her stiletto pumps kicking up clouds of dust and her black purse swinging from the crook of her arm.

Kathryn watched her go with suspicious eyes, petrified the planters might sneak up the steps and bite her in the neck. She shuddered, surprised to see Sylvia making her way up the long drive. This time she didn't come bearing cookies.

"Good morning. Or should I say afternoon? It's almost lunchtime." Sylvia patted her neat straight hair.

"Would you like to come in? I can fix us some ham sandwiches."

"Oh, I don't want to trouble you. I was just passing by and thought I'd drop in and say hello."

"It's no trouble at all, really," Kathryn assured her, wishing with half her heart the old woman would just leave, but the other half wanted, no, *needed* her to stay, so she could sort out last night. She had some questions. Kathryn held the screen door open. "Really, it's no trouble at all. I must eat too, you know."

Kathryn put a fresh mug of coffee in front of Sylvia, the cup she had made for Karen. Sylvia wrapped her hands around it, grateful for the warmth. Kathryn smiled to her impish self. (Sylvia didn't need to know the coffee was recycled. She could just imagine herself as a kitchen fairy with telepathic powers who knew to expect a guest.)

Kathryn sliced sandwiches in half with the carving knife, arranging them on a plate. "What is it you wanted to talk to me about, dear?"

Sylvia admired her skill, which would be wasted on a younger visitor with their iPods and cell phone gadgets. Her shrewd blue eyes glittered.

Brrrrrp! Brrrrrrp! The shrill phone broke Kathryn's train of thought. Her hands slick with mayo, she nodded toward the food. "Would you mind finishing? I have some medium white cheddar in the fridge and some whole dill pickles from my Nanny's kitchen. They'd go wonderfully with those sandwiches."

"Go on, dear, answer the phone and I'll finish up."

"Thank you," Kathryn said, wiping her hands on a green hand towel beside the sink. She picked up the phone on the sixth ring. "Hello?" She walked into the living room for some privacy." She paused. "No, Steve. I told you; the check did not come in the mail." Silence. "Well, how was I supposed to know you changed your number?" Silence. "Well, maybe, your *girlfriend* should have called and given me your new number." Silence.

Meanwhile, Sylvia inspected the blade of the knife, trying to block out the daytime drama in the next room. She ran her finger over the edge of the blade, admiring the craftsmanship. "Trouble?" Sylvia turned, knife in hand.

Kathryn entered the kitchen, her cheeks and neck flushed almost the same color of her dark copper hair, her eyes pinched tight with anger.

"You forgot the pickles. My Nanny makes lovely pickles. Has anything weird ever happened here?"

"Why, heavens, no. What are you talking about?" Sylvia picked up the knife.

"So, you've never had any problem with high school kids on your property at night or heard about The Green Man sect?"

"Why, no. Do you mind if I cut the crusts off my bread? It's a little tough to chew with my dentures." The blade flashed in her hand.

"Go right ahead." Kathryn ate another half sandwich, ravenous. She swallowed again before speaking, wiping a bit of mayo from her upper lip and licking it off her finger. "I've been meaning to ask you more about the family that lived here. I've found something I think belonged to them." Kathryn popped off her stool and ran upstairs.

On the way downstairs, Kathryn tripped and stubbed her sore toe on a step. She swore the book grew hotter than a blasphemer's bible when she saw her own blood running. She spat on her finger and rubbed the blood from her bruised big toe. "This is not my week for toes," she muttered, watching the blood bead around her toenail again. "Oh well, my sandals are old." Kathryn came back to find almost half the sandwiches gone.

"I'm sorry. I'm just so hungry."

Kathryn wondered how Sylvia managed to eat so much when she'd hardly been gone. She slid the book across the counter.

"Oh, my." Sylvia caressed the cover. It felt cool like rain to the touch. "This book must have been beautiful when it was purchased. Very expensive. May I?"

Kathryn nodded.

"Ooo! That smell! It's a shame this book hasn't been taken care of very well. Where did you find it?" She admired the pages with a smile as she turned them.

"It was in the linen closet in my bathroom."

"Well, it certainly didn't belong to the couple here before you. They only lived here for a few months before he got a job in New York."

"So it was the MacArds' book then?" Kathryn's eyes sparkled with interest.

"Oh, yes, yes. It must have been. I suspect it was Collin's book, really." Sylvia closed the book with a solid *thump!* "Collin MacArd was a professor of Celtic literature. His life's passion was anything Celtic to do with his heritage. Why, he even wanted to put on a festival of sorts. This was way, way before Milwaukee even thought of an Irish Fest."

"I was wondering if there was someone I could contact. I'd like to give the book back to his family, or is he still living?"

"I don't know. They sold the house a few years after Margaret died and no one kept in touch." Running her hand over the spine of the mottled green leather, her birdlike eyes brightened. "Why don't you let me take it to my friend Bea at the library? She could clean it up for you and tell you if it's worth something."

"Oh, she can have the darn thing. I don't really need it."

"Are you sure?"

"Yes. The pictures gave me the creeps last night. I'm more than happy to give it a good home."

"Well, if, you're sure." Sylvia checked her watch. "Oh dear, look at the time. I must be going. I have the plumber coming to fix my garbage disposal. I've been too much of a bother already today. I'll just let myself out, dear, and get out of your way." Sylvia shuffled into the foyer, the book in her wrinkled, blue-veined hands.

Kathryn followed, smiling, said, "Have a good afternoon, Sylvia."

Sylvia scanned the cloudy sky. "Looks like it might rain late tonight. Goodbye," she called, waving as she headed down the long, dusty drive.

Kathryn closed the door of her home behind her. *My very own home.* It felt like it now that she'd gotten rid of that infernal book. Divorced at forty—not the end of the world, by any means. In a new fit of furious Steve-induced rage, she decided to attack the remains of the raspberry patch while betrayal and murderous pursuits stoked her blood. With every snip of the gardening shears, Steve lost another limb and died a tragic and slow, torturous death while the ambulance waited, stuck in downtown traffic. "Too bad, so sad, Steve," Kathryn cried, hacking away at the raspberries, leering and pumped with endorphins. She reached to pull on a stubborn raspberry cane,

A large pale pink boulder of unpolished rose quartz sat in the remains of the raspberry patch, and she sat down to rest and inspect her hands. Flat on top, it made the perfect bench. The oaks stirred as a warm breeze picked up, ruffling their leaves. Kathryn stared at the clouds crowding the sun. "It is going to rain later tonight," she said out loud to herself.

***

Sweat crusted between her shoulder blades and her hands stinging, Kathryn opted for an early dinner again, bath, and bed. "My own bed, damnit, where I can read all night long with the lamp on if I please and sleep under a down comforter year-round. Yeah, that's right, Stevie." The words dripped from her lips like the taste of sweet, spilled blood. "I don't have to freeze my ass off anymore because you're always too damn hot." Kathryn rifled through the fridge. She needed to go shopping that weekend. "But," she said to herself, "I still have some fresh garlic, some mozzarella, and those sun-dried tomatoes Steve hates." Kathryn added some olive oil, heated it all in a skillet, and poured it over the leftover pasta she nuked in the microwave. She popped open a Peroni and sank down onto a stool at the breakfast bar, her sore butt screeching in protest as she remembered she also wanted to pick up some cushions. *But I don't have time this weekend.* She sighed, swigging her cold beer and squinching up her face in disgust: not at the Peroni, but at the itemizing of property her attorney needed for the divorce. Then she snorted, the taste of garlic biting and hot on her tongue. *If I'd had to work this hard to get married, maybe I would have thought twice about it.* Who knew getting divorced would be more work than getting married? You get screwed during both, but at least when you're married, you get to enjoy it. She took another swig of Peroni, abandoning her half-eaten pasta as she climbed the stairs to the blessed bathroom and hot water.

She broke into a fit of laughter and then collapsed in tears on the toilet. Bawling, she let the shower run hot, filling the bathroom with steam as she wept. "God, what have I become?" She wiped the steam from the medicine cabinet, staring at her face in the mirror. "I've become one of those bitter divorcees I never wanted to be," she mouthed to her own puffy reflection. She didn't know how long she'd been crying. "Well, let's hope there's still some hot water left, Kathryn." She raised her bottle to her twin in the mirror, chugging long and hard. "Or we'll have to charge his cheating, lying, stinking ass for emotional distress too." Kathryn yanked the rattling shower curtain shut, relaxing her jaw as she let the hot water run over her tired muscles and hurried to wash as the water turned frigid. Shaking, dripping wet, and still pissed, Kathryn vowed to drink herself towards happiness tonight. Wrapping a giant towel around her slender frame, she stalked downstairs to get another Peroni and returned upstairs to her bedroom with three. She guzzled one with angry gusto before passing out from physical and emotional exhaustion, still wrapped in her towel, her hair wet and unkempt, sprawled long-legged across the width of the bed with her head facing the bedroom window.

***

The moon shone white through the patches of oaks after the storm. Kathryn awoke, her throat raw with grief and her tongue fuzzy from beer. All her muscles tensed, pulling straighter than broomsticks as she investigated her backyard. She let the empty beer bottle fall from her cramped hand and snatched the white robe from the floor, allowing the damp towel to slip to her feet now that she wore the robe.

"It's not an animal. It's not a man. It's… What is it?" With trembling lips, Kathryn watched it walk with a jerky wooden gait. In her half-dazed state, she shook her hair from her eyes, squinting. The figure in the moonlight turned its tombstone gaze to her bedroom window. *The Green Man.* Kathryn gasped and took two steps back from the window, as if the darkness of her bedroom could protect her. "No, I don't believe in monsters." Her fingers clung to the white robe she wore, hugging her body tight. "This robe is real. I am real. The horned creature isn't." In the moonlight its white teeth glinted like coins. "No!" Kathryn rushed to the window, grasping the ledge. "This," she cried in fear, "this is real." She grabbed the ledge harder. "That thing out there is not real. It's the booze—that's all—the booze! But still…"

A flood of rage crackled within her bones as she ran barefoot down the stairs, through the kitchen, and out the back door into her yard, her heels slapping the mud, soggy leaves sticking to her feet and calves like garden slugs, mud splattering onto her pale legs and the hem of her white robe. "You are *not* real! And I will *not* be scared out of my own house! You hear me? Damn you, do you hear me," she cried to the monster, watching it teeter towards her. *This, this monster, this jumble of living vines is not real,* she thought, silent, rage burning in her bones.

"Kathryn," the Green Man whispered in a soft, husky voice. "Come to me." Kathryn froze. The thing opened its reedy arms, revealing its chest, a tangle of snarled vines of green life twisting around and down its torso in a thick web. Oak leaves shivered around its horrible green leering face, the mask of its face drier than an acorn's, cracking as it spoke.

"Kathryn." In its gnarled hands it clasped a scythe, the silver light of the moon rippling over the blade like water. Silent, The Green Man removed its mask, revealing Sylvia's shining green painted face.

Something black, twisted, and feral snapped within Kathryn, and with a primal shout that shook even the moon nestled in amongst her blanket of stars, Kathryn charged Sylvia, knocking her down, her stilts clattering as she fell in a tangle of robes of fake greenery, the scythe flying from Sylvia's grasp. Fast, lithe, and fierce, Kathryn retrieved the scythe from the ground, the handle now slippery with mud.

Cackling, Sylvia crawled away through the muck on her belly to the pink stone, the mica flecks glinting in the moonlight, her stilts still attached to her feet, dragged through the muddy ground in deep gouges. "You're not worthy of living here amongst us, Kathryn. You're not good enough for him."

"Good enough for who?"

"The Green Man."

"So you thought you'd scare me away? Is that what happened to the other family before me? Is there really a Green Man sect?" Kathryn wielded the scythe over her.

Gasping, her voice no louder than dry leaves in the wind, Sylvia commanded Kathryn. "Do it," she shouted, wetting her lips with old woman spittle as she hugged the boulder, her tiny frame quaking. "Do it, Kathryn! Use your anger! Offer me to the God of the Forest! Let me be his bride!"

Kathryn towered over Sylvia, her chest heaving, the scythe at her side, her hand caked with mud. "Yes," she howled, hot tears of vengeance rushing down her cheeks. Kathryn's shoulders trembled as she raised the scythe over Sylvia's crouched and quaking body. "Yes," she hollered, louder still, her voice a turbulent volcano erupting in her throat. The anger, the grief, and humiliation, the betrayal, and the disgust she'd suffered in the past six months swelled up within her; the sleepless nights; the fear of being alone; the fear of being vulnerable poured loose, gushing forth from her throat in a hot, raw roar. "Damn you to hell, Steven! Damn you to hell, Sylvia! This is *my* house! This is *my* life!" The scythe fell swift. Sylvia jeered and writhed, her blood spraying thick and hot over Kathryn's bare toes, her calves and her dirty white robe splattered with scarlet and mud as she swung the scythe with a vicious glint in her eye. *No, this woman, this woman will not take from me what is mine. And neither will Steve*, she thought. And with every downward stroke, Sylvia cried out, "It was supposed to be you, Kathryn, but my blood will do," until her ecstasy bled from her now quiet body, and she lay like a crushed heap of rose petals, bruised and red and wet. She sacrificed her blood to the ancient Green Man like her ancestors before her and, perhaps, he would live again.

SILENCE HAS A COLOR

The women's unit on the first floor of the Peabody Psychological Institute nestled like a spider in the old east wing of the repurposed mansion. A grand structure constructed of yellow pressed brick and carved limestone; the two-story classical mansion built in 1897 was now part of the sprawling labyrinth of buildings owned by the Lycena Healthcare system. A dramatic portico flanked by four fluted columns greeted patients. Tall oak trees lined the red brick way on either side like obedient stewards. On the night I arrived at the hospital, only three rooms lay empty. Luckily, I wasn't on the extreme ward reserved for the really troubled patients. I counted nine rooms, mine being at the end of a long hallway with a large window up high facing what I assumed was an old side garden, from when I came in through the ward's doors. The hallway smelled of a mix of disinfectant and something savory, possibly chicken pot pie. My stomach growled as I was ushered into a small room with a single bed placed on the outside wall. I remember that placement well because it was so hard to get to sleep.

The mattress, thinner than a plush dog bed, did nothing to relieve the dull aching of my sleep-deprived joints, and though I was given three standard issue cotton hospital blankets, they were of little comfort against the perpetual chill of Room 5. The chill, a hungry, relentless animal, sank its teeth into my backside, refusing to relinquish its grasp, though I slept in sweatpants, two pairs of thick boot socks, and doubled my sweatshirts, pulling a white knit hat down over my fine hair to keep my head warm. I covered my nose with my blankets, shifting painfully on the narrow mattress. Outside, the wind churned up dirt and dry leaves, pitching them against the window with resentful force. The small ward was silent, the only sound the staccato *plink, plink, plink* of the faucet in the bathroom.

I turned over on my right side, facing the bare wall, and scrunched my eyes closed against the tiny yellow rectangle of the nightlight. I imagined the horizontal slits of light as the visor of a menacing alien robot, emitting angry yellow slashes. Snot dripped from the tip of my nose; it was so cold, colder than I remembered upon entering my room an hour earlier.

I stirred and got up to pee, noting the screws fastening the toilet to the wall covered by flat protective metal plates, impossible to pry away from the wall. The word "hi" was scratched into the bathroom mirror. I tapped my pale reflection with a broken nail. The mirror wasn't made of glass. Part of me realized the absurdity of my reflection watching me from sleep-haunted eyes, wearing a knit cap with cat ears on a psych ward of all places, but most of me felt numb, removed from this version of reality.

I sighed, the soft susurration of air swallowed by the bathroom. My pink traveling toothbrush and my toothpaste made a sad and lonely pair beside the sink. I'd placed them on a cheap paper towel rectangle, now wet because I didn't trust the odd yellow stain beside the standard hospital bar soap. The stain on the sink was shaped like Patrick the starfish from *SpongeBob Squarepants.* I smiled and my bottom lip cracked, oozing bright crimson on my peeling flesh. My front teeth worried the small split in my skin, the salty taste of my blood on my tongue a familiar lover's kiss.

I couldn't shake the cold. It wrapped me in its icy embrace, reminding me of a game I used to play as a child, a challenge I set myself. How long could I stay outside playing in the snow in the middle of a Wisconsin winter? Until my toes burned? Until my fingertips screamed for a warm mug of hot chocolate to thaw them? When my cheeks turned red as meat and the bitter wind tore tears from the corners of my eyes? Right then, I noticed the tears running down my face. I touched my right hand to my cheek and anointed my tongue with the salty water to remind myself I was still alive.

Hi. My fingertips worried the etching. I shivered. What was the girl, no, the young woman thinking that left this message behind? Was it a declaration of existence? A desperate plea for attention or a mark to let me know I'm not alone? Someone's claim to life? A reminder they were still human, not some injured animal locked away in a cage? I couldn't know. The *plink, plink, plink* of the faucet interrupted my thoughts. I realized I'd been standing in front of the mirror for at least ten minutes, I thought. I would not be able to sleep without help. I felt weak and dependent, but I needed that pill. I shuffled off to the nurse's station for an Ativan and soon sweet relief flooded my body, the tight snake of anxiety in my stomach uncoiling into a warm mush of taffy. I curled into a ball and slept.

I awoke the next morning, shivering. My nose told me breakfast had already been served. Because I was new on the ward and in shock, they allowed me to sleep in, since I came in late that night, and held my breakfast for me. New patients generally rested the first day or two before joining group therapy because the change from home was so startling. It was Saturday in the real world. The drowned sunlight declaring winter's onset filled the courtyard, though I couldn't see the courtyard because of how high up the windows were positioned. My eyelids felt heavy and the corners of my mouth sticky from sleep and lack of moisture. I let out a tiny sigh as I shed my clothes and stepped into the shower. The water was blessedly hot, not freezing as expected, and I stood under that stream of bliss for a long time, visualizing a fountain of warmth soaking into my aching bones.

"Hi," a voice whispered, so close, I could feel hot breath in my left ear. I jumped and almost slipped and landed on my ass, but at the last moment steadied myself. I poked my head out of the shower, but nobody was there. A nauseating sweet scent of oranges stirred about me, and I gagged, acid flooding the back of my throat as my nose stung. That smell. I *hated* that smell. It was the citrus shampoo I used in high school; the shampoo my mom brought me when I spent the holidays locked up in the kids' ward of some posh psych hospital. The mirrors weren't made of glass. I remember my roommate; I'll call her "Shana" for privacy's sake; Shana with her journal of scars etched into her arms; Shana who would only wear long sleeves so nobody could see her ugly truth. *Shana.* So damaged, but so cool to my thirteen-year-old self. I wanted to be badass like her; to not give a shit about anything; to not feel ashamed, humiliated, and broken, or like a failure to my parents. *Shana.*

Shana sneaked contraband into our room, a metal piece from a pen. The staff made a grave error, and nobody ever found out how Shana got the pen. She took it apart. I never found out where she hid the rest of it. I should have asked. I should have turned her in, because Shana was on suicide watch just like me and neither of us were allowed pens or pencils. They were weapons we could use against ourselves, but Shana, she'd been in and out of hospitals since she was eleven. And she was fifteen then, older, and cooler than I could ever hope to become. She didn't sleep in nightshirts with cuddly teddy bears or wear saddle shoes her mom bought. She was all hard angles and grit. She'd make even a pencil feel fat. She only liked to eat white foods on Thursday and didn't give a flying fuck, her exact words, that her uncle raped her when she was seven. Shana was badass. Tough. Strong. In this world there were suckers and survivors. Which one was Shana? A survivor. You're right, my friend. That's why she took that piece of metal and scratched *hello* into our bathroom mirror. She said it was so when she looked at herself every day, she'd be reminded she was still human. Still *somebody*. But now that I'm older, I know she did it for me, for me to remember her.

Shana was only my roommate for two days before we were separated. I got a room of my own. They said she was a bad influence. The darkness crouched on my chest like a demon intent on taking my soul without Shana's soft snoring beside me, keeping me safe. One day, after they moved Shana out of my room, she slashed her wrists open with that metal pen piece. I didn't see her after that. She was transferred off the children's ward. I lost my best friend there. In there you make friends quickly because you bond against the staff. I was a leftover now, left with the rejects or, as I sarcastically named them after my favorite movie, *The Breakfast Club*, my bunch of "misfit fiends."

I thought about offering this anecdote during our morning group share, but I didn't know who I could trust in here yet. There's always one girl on the ward that seems perfectly sane, aside from being on a locked psych ward. She's the one you must worry about getting close to here. She seems like your friend, but really, she's just a pot waiting to boil. A watched pot may not boil, as the saying goes, but if you're not cautious, you'll get burned when it overflows.

"Why are there covers on all the switches and outlets in my room?" asked the new girl.

Sandra, who introduced herself to me earlier, looked up from her ball of yarn and knitting needles because she'd been there for months and was on good behavior. She could only use them supervised and a nurse sat by her the entire time. "So you can't take them off and make a weapon or electrocute yourself. Everything in here is idiot proof."

I stared at the dry erase board behind her. It read: *Welcome to Martha Stewart hell.* I laughed.

"The shower curtains are velcroed to the tiles so you can't hang yourself. They won't hold any weight. The blinds are between high windows. No razors. No picture hangers. Only foam square double tape. The mirrors aren't made of glass. You can't break them and slit your wrists. You have no bathroom doors, only a velcroed curtain, so you can't lock yourself in any place. You aren't allowed hand lotion with alcohol because a detoxing alcoholic might want to drink it, though why'd you want to drink something that smells like an apple farted is beyond me. You must be a newbie. You'll learn," said another woman. She could hardly be more than eighteen, with her shiny fresh skin and braces.

"Why isn't there a chair in my room? I have a desk," New Girl asked.

Good question. I'd wondered the same damn thing myself. We all waited like obedient sheep for our leader to respond.

Dawn, our group counselor for the day, cleared her throat and tapped her foot on the tile. She wore New Balance walking shoes, brand new, judging from the lack of dirt. "There was an incident involving a chair on the ward last week. And it was decided that chairs are no longer safe items in patient rooms."

"Did someone figure out a way to kill themselves?" Sandra asked, glancing up from the black afghan she was knitting. "Good for them!"

New Girl looked horrified. She'd introduced herself earlier and shared that it was her "first time." "And that's a good thing?" New Girl asked. Her voice climbed an octave with the last word. I could tell she was a Type A overachiever by the way she dressed: a young, hip college graduate, dark jeggings, black shoes without laces. She carried a *Good News Bible* and a floral journal with *My Thoughts* scrawled across the cover in large, elegant cursive. *Uck*. She'd ask too many questions and if any bad shit went down like Sandra trying to start a fight, I knew this chick wouldn't have my back, front, or side. She'd probably run and hide. I spent the rest of group listening to the young girl that resembled Barbie's sister, Skipper, talk about her extreme guilt over shoplifting.

***

I never knew silence had a color, but that night it did—grey. A heavy grey blanket of silence hung over my room, seeping into the atmosphere like a damp November fog with craven, searching fingers. I burrowed deeper into my nest of hospital blankets, wiggling my toes for warmth. The shower gushed on at full force. I felt powerless, every muscle frozen, taut. The hairs on the back of my neck—the link to our earlier ancestors, I'd once read—had already risen or they would have leapt to attention now, surely. I remembered an article explaining how tiny muscles connected to each hair follicle contracted, allowing our skin to trap as much heat as possible. I tried to calm myself with this fact and as quickly as the shower turned on, it stopped. I breathed in through my nose and out through my mouth, attempting to ground myself. The taste of maple syrup from dinner was thick in my throat.

I was startled and swallowed as my bedroom door popped open. "Group," a nurse I hadn't met yet chirped. "You've got two minutes to make it there."

I rinsed the furry feeling from my mouth, conscious while I combed my hair that the bathroom felt occupied, but nobody else was there. Like a ninny, I checked behind the shower curtain and found no one. No person who had written a note on the mirror, anyway.

***

Later that night, I lay in bed, shivering again. Thankfully, the night nurse managed to find me a few more blankets. They weren't much help, but it was better than before. I'd discovered how to turn off the nightlight earlier that evening. I never slept well in unfamiliar settings away from home or in a room with a light. Only a faint strip of light showed beneath my bedroom door.

It was past midnight when I heard a commotion across the hall. I thought it was Sandra arguing with the night nurse. I sat up, pulling a blanket around me like a granny shawl, and crept to my door. I had just placed my cheek against the door when a soft whisper tickled my left ear. "Hi," it said.

I jumped, banging my right knee on the door and my head. *Ow!*

I gimped to the bathroom and turned on the light, thinking to grab an Advil, but then I remembered where I was staying. *How could I have forgotten?* I stood before the mirror, wincing in the fluorescent light.

I ran my fingertip over the greeting etched in the mirror, watching my reflection trace the word. The cool, shallow indentation soothed me for a split second, but then the shower came rushing on again and I nearly lit out of my socks. My breath stuck in my throat like ice, and I yanked back the curtain to find an empty white-tiled stall. Water dripped from the showerhead. *Surely it was something to do with air pressure in the pipes. It couldn't be haunted. Right?* The showerhead was warm. I ran my hand around the drain. It was also warm and *wet.* My eyes traveled back to the mirror. And I remembered Shana. *What happened to her?*

I turned off the light and padded back to bed, my knee and forehead throbbing, the tip of my nose frozen as I pulled my covers up to my ears, eyes wide open, ears straining to place every sound, the *plink, plink, plink* of the leaky faucet and the rattle of the wind against my windows. The shower ran on and off two more times that night. I imagined Shana stumbling towards me, her wrists held out to me, revealing sickle-shaped scars winking at me in the moonlight. I could almost smell the sweet pink bubblegum I used to chew in high school. *What was it called? Bazooka! The one with the comics printed on waxy wrappers.* The smell of my youth mingled with the faint scent of bleach and industrial detergent wafting off the blankets as I inhaled beneath the covers.

I wondered about the chair incident. *Had someone died in this room?* I remembered how Robin Williams was found. *Maybe something similar with a sheet? Not a belt. They didn't permit belts or shoelaces for that exact reason. If you wanted to die while you were here, you had to really earn it. But how long would you need to asphyxiate?* I had no idea. I'd always favored something less painful like pills or slitting my wrists in the bathtub and just floating away into the warmth, comforted by the rocking motion of the water, almost like returning to the womb. Macabre horrors of bulging, bloody eyes, blackened and swollen tongues, and mottled faces seized my imagination.

I'd also read an article by a neuropsychologist explaining poltergeist activity such as the shower gushing on by itself and auditory phenomena. In times of extreme stress, usually during adolescence when hormones come into play and affect cognitive functioning, a person could act like a conduit, a stored battery, discharging energy into the atmosphere. It was also documented after head trauma or taking certain medications, when patients reported hallucinations with concussions. Both a hard hit to the head and the introduction of a new chemical compound to the nervous system could result in what is often explained as poltergeist activity. But could a ghost possess someone else's body? Could they harness enough of your energy? Essentially, we were all giant computers, jumbles of signals firing off neurons in our brains every second. *If a poltergeist could cause objects to move, lights to go on, and faucets to turn on and off, dishes flying out of cupboards and televisions turning themselves on, why not? Had Shana come to haunt me? But what about the first "Hi" in the shower before I hit my head? What was going on?*

I rubbed the tender bump on the side of my forehead. *What if I had simply been Aliced, for lack of a better verb, through my own looking glass into a new reality?* I did believe in alternate universes. While I loathed Ashton Kutcher, the Hollywood blockbuster *The Butterfly Effect* had done a more than adequate job explaining the existence of alternate universes and chaos theory; a one-minute change could result in an infinite number of realities. *Was I living this theory? I didn't know.* My thoughts were sluggish from lack of sleep, I was disoriented from the Ativan, but my brain worked differently than others and it took a huge dose of downers to knock me out because I had gone through a lot of surgeries, so my mind was just relaxed. I couldn't have a large enough dose to help me sleep. I was nineteen, technically still a young adult, old enough to vote. And I *had* hit my head earlier on the door. There was the always the possibility I really was going crazy, but Dr. Liebaum reassured me earlier that patients that are crazy rarely actually *worry* about being crazy. This was only a small comfort at this moment. Anxiety makes the worst bed companion.

***

Morning came sooner than my bloodshot eyes liked. Judging by the matching set of heavy luggage under my eyes, it was going to be one hell of a day. "Hi." I traced the word with my index finger, reassuring myself I was still here. Still present in this glorious little shithole. *Yay!* I'd get to spend another day listening to Skipper confess her shoplifting crimes.

"We're all mad here," I whispered to my reflection through a Cheshire Cat grin.

And that's when I noticed the chair behind me in the mirror, honey blond and scarred, the same color as the other furniture in my room. *But there was no chair in my room. How could this be?* I peered into the mirror, leaning in, clutching the edge of the porcelain sink on both sides, trying to ground myself in the present by identifying five sensations as Dr. Liebaum taught me.

"Hi," I heard her whisper in my ear. I smelled bubblegum and citrus shampoo. The sweet and tart combination roiled my stomach.

"Shana?"

"Uh-huh." I blinked twice, gulped, closed my eyes, and counted backwards to ten. I tried to will away the bloated and bruised face peering back at me from the mirror.

"You aren't really here." I touched my cheeks, a sepulchral chill leeching into my fingertips.

"Oh, but I *am* here because *you* are." Shana pulled her lips back in a rictus.

"No." I traced the greeting in the mirror with my fingertip over and over, willing myself to return to present reality. "You're not here. You're *not* real. Are you *real*?" I paused and leaned in closer, my breath fogging the mirror. *I* was real. *This* was real.

"Am I real?" Shana's corpse stared at me from the mirror.

I pulled back. My reflection mimicked me. But it wasn't the adult me any longer. It was the thirteen-year-old me; skinny me with Guess jeans and braces and owlish wire-rimmed glasses taking up half my face. I watched myself pull a sharpened piece of metal from my sock. And then my breath hitched as I watched the thirteen-year-old me etch "hello" in the mirror. Then I pushed up the sleeves of my white sweater with deliberate care. I did not hesitate as I dug the metal into my flesh, yanking it fast and hard from the wrist to my elbow. So much blood, so fast, and so bright! The metal piece fell from my hand as I staggered to my bed. I was always good at grifting items without anyone noticing and Sandra had been distracted, as had the nurse when another patient threw a fit over the art therapy class coming up.

"Katie!" I heard my name as my pulse beat loudly in my ears. Was I dying? Was this real or had I already died? Was I a ghost? Was Shana a ghost? Was I Shana?

My tiny room bustled with people. I was getting colder, so cold, and so tired. Just like all those years ago. The light seemed further away, voices softer and muffled. The color of silence filled my vision, everything tinged grey, but from my bed, I could see a wink of sea-green metal on the bathroom floor, the Crayola color I loved as a kid.

The last thing I heard was Sandra's voice. "I didn't even know my knitting needle was missing!"

You must always watch out for those girls that get too friendly too fast, Sandra. They're always up to something. I smiled and sighed as I felt a warm, strong hand grasp my arm.

THE WITCH OF FOX POINT

The 1925 bungalow watched over the strange menagerie of cement statues adorned with driftwood, rocks, and bits of beach glass. Slashes of moonlight broke through the clouds, shattering the darkness of the bare trees towering over the house. The wind whipped through Anne's hair and froze the tip of her nose and cheeks. Snot dripped from her nose, and she wiped it with the sleeve of her sweatshirt, the scent of petrichor and Lake Michigan strong in her nostrils.

"Anne, come on," her boyfriend Jimmy complained. He knelt in front of what many called "The Witch's House" but was really Mary Nohl's Lake Michigan artist retreat. The legend says Nohl murdered her husband and threw him into the lake. His body was never recovered. Mary Nohl lived a solitary life as an artist and became known by the locals as "The Witch of Fox Point." She was buried in her sculpture garden and the best time to contact her was during the full moon on the anniversary of her death.

The waves pummeled the breakwater. The spray launched itself towards the bungalow, seeking welcome from an old friend, but only made it as far as the erosion link of the cliff the small cottage crouched on.

Moonlight reflected off the eerie monolith stone heads sprouting up from the earth. Where the pine trees grew, shadows rippled like water over the bodies of the fish and people on the blue and green bas reliefs of the bungalow.

Anne stood barefoot in front of the chain-link fence topped with rusted barbed wire. The electricity of the coming storm raced like fire through her veins and her nipples hardened, the tiny hairs on the back of her neck erect. She licked her lips.

"Anne."

"Yes, Jimmy." She knelt beside him on the hard blacktop. Jimmy was a good fuck, but not a top student in school. He knew how to give good head and he didn't kiss like a sloppy fish. Did she really think this summoning ceremony would work? No. She sighed and resigned herself to an evening of sexless disappointment. Anne was used to these ceremonies, spending a lot of time in her grandmother's company. Anne's grandmother was a witch, but Anne's mother had raised her as an atheist. Anne came from a long line of witches dating back before the Salem Witch Trials, but she didn't feel magick in her blood.

Anne took the piece of chalk from Jimmy's sweaty outstretched palm and sketched a pentagram in bold strokes big enough to lay a body inside. She placed the stone canopic jar in the center of the pentagram, unaware what offering sat inside it. Jimmy lit a black taper and dripped candlewax on the first point of the pentagram, sticking the taper upright in the pool of wax. He lit the next and repeated the routine four times. The candles' flames drifted upwards as they grew taller. The smell of candlewax filled the air. Anne caressed the cover of the canopic jar.

Jimmy grabbed her hand and faced her. She could smell the sugary sweet gum on his breath as he whispered, "Let's do this." He squeezed her fingers, mashing her knuckles together hard and sending shooting pains through her hand.

Anne pulled the crumpled loose-leaf sheet from her jeans pocket. The blue lines glowed with intensity in the moonlight. Licking her lips again, she steadied her shaky hands and held the incantation between them. They tilted their faces up like moonflowers to the lady in the sky shining down on them as they spoke:

Mortuous cujus tempora transierunt da ei unum ultimum depraehendo hoc objectum i largiri cum animo tuo Nuuit iter tuum et auxilio Dei ad hoc vol out fiat mihi.

The wind howled like a banshee at the site of a massacre and snuffed out all the candles at once.

***

On the trendy east side of Milwaukee, the antiques and collectibles store Enchanted Endings hunkered between an old-fashioned pharmacy on the corner and a small accountant's office on the right. McKay, the owner, hunched over his cherry hardwood desk, papers strewn like dead leaves across the top. A circle of light from the green glass banker's lamp highlighted the old rotary phone as he dialed Malcolm's number with a No. 2 pencil. Next to the phone a dark blue stone lay on a black velvet cloth.

"Hello?"

"Malcolm, it's McKay at Enchanted Endings. I've acquired a piece that might interest you."

"Yes?"

"Are you familiar with King Solomon's ring?"

"The Seal of Solomon?"

"Yes. A young lady recently inherited her grandfather's estate. He served in World War II under General George S. Patton. Her grandfather's company was assigned to guard the Nazi treasure the Americans recovered in the Merkers Salt Mines. He helped himself to a little souvenir, a stone, a very valuable and powerful stone from King Solomon's ring." McKay practically heard Malcolm drooling as he spoke.

"And you have this stone in your possession?"

"Indeed I do. And I am prepared to offer it to you for a pretty penny, my friend. Are you in the market for a new antiquity, Malcolm?" McKay twirled the pencil in his left hand, staring down at the dark cobalt blue lapis lazuli carving.

The stone was the richest, darkest blue with fine gold veins throughout. An expert from the Milwaukee Public Museum had appraised the gem. It came from an area of the Afghanistan mountains noted for its fine specimens. If it were of lesser value, it would be greenish in color, containing too much pyrite. This stone would fetch a hefty sum; McKay's green eyes sparked with pleasure.

The story of the Seal was as colorful as the stone. King Solomon's birth name was Jedidiah, meaning "friend of God." Later in life, he was named Solomon, which meant "King of Peace." When he saw precious gems stolen during the building of his temple, King Solomon intuitively knew it was a supernatural event and prayed to God to find him the evil spirit responsible for the theft. Immediately, Archangel Michael appeared with a lapis lazuli ring bestowing upon King Solomon the power to control demons and the power to summon genies and speak to animals and flowers. On the seal God carved an eight-rayed star. In that star was the hexagonal seal and within that were carved the four letters of God's name. Following Christian legend, it was believed to be the only holy weapon useful against the impending apocalypse, residing in the darkest chambers of the Vatican, or it did until WWII.

How Hitler acquired the Seal of Solomon, McKay could only guess. Hitler had been very interested in the occult and various religious artifacts he believed contained great power. It was an invaluable treasure, but for the right price, McKay would sell it off the books.

***

Blocks away from Enchanted Endings sat a modest two-story Queen Anne Victorian converted into the well-used East Side funeral home Tranquil Pastures. It was a family-owned business going back a few generations. The home oozed character with its spindle-work, patterned wood shingles, and a set of red brick steps leading to a plum-colored front door adorned with a bright brass handle and mail slot. White lace curtains were drawn across the front windows. The main floor of the funeral parlor consisted of two viewing rooms, an office, a spacious lobby, the casket showroom and bathrooms. Downstairs had been converted into the morgue and cosmetic preparation of bodies for viewing. One could imagine the attic, used only for storage, was fashioned with the appropriate number of cobwebs, mice, and perhaps a sleeping bat or two in the corner eaves.

The lobby carpet showed fresh vacuum tracks. Oil paintings of floral arrangements and peaceful riverbanks hung in gold gilt frames on the grey floral wallpaper. The dark mahogany woodwork shone with years of loving polish.

Ethel Idris sat at her dark hardwood desk in her cream Queen Anne wingbacked chair, a fire crackling in the fireplace. Dried floral arrangements and bits of Victorian ephemeral whimsy, complimenting the muted greys and creams, perched on the mantel in ornate silver frames with not a speck of dust. Ethel sighed and leaned over her green-bound accounting book with a magnifying glass, squinting behind her bifocals as she struggled to read her assistant's scraggly handwriting. She sniffled and drew her powder blue cashmere sweater closer, pulling a pressed white handkerchief with curling green leaves from her pocket. Soothing harp music played over the sound system. The ticking of the mantel clock, along with the rumbling in her stomach, reminded her she missed supper. Perhaps her sister left a plate of meatloaf warming in the oven at home.

She closed the book and set it aside, turning off the crystal lamp and the sound system. Slipping on her grey kitten heels, she began checking the rest of the first floor. The phone rang, startling her from her own thoughts as she turned off the gas fireplace.

"Yes, Alicia." A pause. "Yes, I'll be home within the next hour. I just have to finish Mr. Chandler's makeup and hair for the funeral tomorrow." Another pause. "Yes, the florist will be delivering the arrangements an hour before the family arrives." Another pause. "Mr. Chandler's sister decided upon the classical piano medley we discussed." Another pause. "No, I'll finish the books for the month tomorrow after the morning service. I'm almost done." Another pause. "Yes, I love you too, dear sister. I'll be home soon."

Ethel jumped as the wind picked up and bare branches scraped against the side of the house. She was a tiny woman with petite feet and a coifed silver French twist. Her round, pleasant face was smooth of wrinkles at fifty-four years of age. She wore her nails short and unpolished because of her cosmetic work. A tiny gold cross glinted around her neck and as she moved from her cozy office, the sweet scent of her cosmetic powder floated behind her on a warm draft of air.

***

"Anne."

"What Jimmy?" She couldn't believe she'd wasted a good evening in the cold trying to summon Mary Nohl's ghost. She could have been home, curled up with a book and a mug of peppermint tea. Anne shivered.

"Do you hear that?"

"Hear what, Jimmy?"

"That crying."

Anne sat motionless, listening to the rhythmic waves crashing against the breakwater, and then she heard it. A low keening. A herd of cows over the water. The moon broke through the cloud cover that had appeared without warning and shone over the frantic waves rushing to shore.

And then she saw them walking on top of the water.

Impossible.

Hundreds of skeletons shambled forward when they should have sunk in the waves, their aged bones slimy, slick with algae and glistening with duckweed, milfoil and eelgrass clinging to their torsos and hanging from their eye sockets with crusted zebra mussels nestled in their rib cages. Some skeletons dragged rusty fishing traps and frayed shipping ropes behind them. Tiny silver alewives and other fish flopped from their yawning skulls as they gnashed their teeth. Dirty water, sand stirred up with the waves, poured from their eye sockets. More and more skeletons rose from the lake.

Lake Michigan is a vengeful mistress. Many a sailor and many a ship sink beneath her waters never to be seen again. It's estimated that 1,500 of the 6,000 shipwrecks attributed to the Great Lakes occurred on Lake Michigan, some dating back hundreds of years. One of the most notorious wrecks was the wooden ship the *Lady Elgin*, which sank on

September 8, 1860. Over three hundred people and fifty cows in the cargo hold lost their lives that day, which accounted for the giant cow skeletons striding over the rough waves, mooing and bellowing in distress, eelgrass strung across their steer horns like Christmas lights.

"Fuck," Jimmy said.

"Fuck," Anne said, as they rose to their feet, backing away from Mary Nohl's house and the advancing skeletal army marching up the breakwater and clambering over the chain link fence into the sculpture garden.

Beneath the sharp drop to the breakwater a red light pulsed on and off from the storm sewer drain; it rotated like a maniacal lighthouse beacon. The ground vibrated and rumbled.

"What is going on?" Jimmy stumbled backwards, gaping in horror as a pack of coyotes arrived and sat in a silent circle, their noses sniffing the night air, ivory-colored teeth bared. Yellow eyes flashing like swamp fire in the dark, they turned their sentinel gaze upon Anne and Jimmy, running as fast as they could westward, up Beach Drive, up the huge hill to the safety of Lake Drive. As they fled, a teeming horde of rats scurried over their feet and up their pant legs, up their torsos and to their shoulders. Jimmy cried out in pain as needle sharp teeth sank into his earlobe. The rats overtook him and his body disappeared beneath a squirming blanket of fur. Anne perched on a giant white boulder near a pine tree, scrambling into the safety of its branches as she panted, her face slick with a sheen of sweat, stinking of animal fear. She watched, helpless, as the rats ripped and tore at Jimmy's clothes, shredding his flesh. Bare bone glistened beneath red sinew and muscle. One rat bit into his eye and ran away with its gelatinous prize connected to a bundle of jiggling nerves. A large red gash in his jaw revealed Jimmy's teeth still grinding. Another rat yanked out his windpipe and for a minute it looked comical, like the crazed rodent carried a flopping cartilaginous snorkel as it dashed into some bushes. The rats departed as one beast, leaving a soggy, soaking red mess. Jimmy lay, a heap of crumpled flesh, no longer recognizable. A coyote tore off his left foot with savage ferocity and ran away with its meat.

Anne howled, biting into her fist as she sobbed. She mulled it over. Stay in the tree or make a run for it. She decided to scamper down the tree and grabbed a large fallen branch to wield as a club, starting back up the steep hill toward help. As she fled, she noticed a black cat sitting on the porch of a mansion, cleaning its paws with efficiency. What was going on? It truly was hell on earth. The ritual she and Jimmy performed had opened a gateway and the dead were alive and hungry. Anne jumped as another black cat ran across her path and hissed at her, its back arched in typical Halloween fashion.

***

The grand wrought iron gates guarding Forest Home Cemetery stood open, the tall stone pillars glowing in the moonlight. In her coffin, Mary Louise Nohl awoke, preserved as well as the day she died three days before Christmas in 2001. Her brick red sweater and her spring green dress with the Peter Pan collar were as straight and crisp as when she was laid to rest beside her siblings, Max, Emma, and Frederick, the infant who lived for only a year. Her grey hair was swept back from her face. It perched like a silver fox on her head, not stirring in the wind as she shambled along in her comfortable brown loafers, loose dirt and earthworms cascading from her head and shoulders, mud caked under her few remaining fingernails not broken as she punched through the top of her casket and clawed her way to the fresh night air. A smear of dirt graced one heavily blushed cheek and a tear on the top of her right-hand leaked embalming fluid, revealing colorless flesh. The wire keeping her lower jaw held shut snapped and her mouth fell open. Her dry, lifeless tongue flopped from her mouth like a fish as she moaned and followed a parade of corpses in various stages of decay and dress from the cemetery grounds. Her eyelids, once glued shut, flapped like flabby chicken skin, ripped and torn.

Mary Nohl was driven only by a gnawing hunger. She had no memory of her previous life, but oddly, the image of a great body of water winked in and out of her atrophied brain. Guided only by the hive mind of the others, she shuffled out of the cemetery. *Food, food, food.* The thought beat like a drum inside her belly.

***

Beethoven played as Ethel sat on a black pleather stool before one of the two embalming tables. She had not made it home for supper in the past hour because she'd made an emergency stop at Fox Run Estates, the assisted living community. Maeve Bellweather lay on one of the tables hooked up to the embalming machine, which hissed as blood pumped out into the special embalming collection system installed between the two embalming tables. Ethel's fountain pen lay on a business form next to Mr. Chandler's body. She was going over the final checklist for the service tomorrow at 9AM. The clinical lighting did nothing to warm Mr. Chandler's complexion. He was laid out in a black suit, slit up the back for easy dressing purposes. Ethel dipped her brush into a bit more mortuary cosmetic illusion crème to add more glow to the highlights on Mr. Chandler's face. She was almost out of the lightest color in the standard Caucasian kit and would need to order more soon. The burn on Mr. Chandler's cheek still showed a bit, so she used some Restor spray, which created a matte surface for the cosmetics to stick to better. Then she took out her hair curler to gently curl his bangs away from his forehead, as he wore his hair in life.

She reached for her pen and drew back in horror. She blinked. It must be a trick of her tired eyes. She glanced away and then back again. Yes, the pen was oozing what looked like blood. Curious. She picked it up between two fingers and carried it to the bathroom off the embalming room.

Upstairs, unbeknownst to Ethel, large spots of blood burst like balloons on the fine silk wallpaper and dribbled to the floor in the lobby where the muted grey carpeting guzzled it like a greedy newborn. The stains began to spread away from the wall. In the first-floor guest bathrooms, rivers of crimson gushed from the faucets, spilling in a thick viscous pool onto the black and white herringbone-patterned floor. The toilets in each stall flushed with a giant *whoosh!* and blood geysers erupted from the bowls, splashing the white subway-tiled walls behind them. Cracks spiderwebbed from the center of the mirrors above the sinks. The overhead fluorescent lights buzzed and flickered on, then off, then on again, before the bulbs exploded in a shower of frosted glass.

On the mantle in Ethel's office, all the glass shattered at once in the silver picture frames as the phone on her desk began ringing.

***

A few blocks away, Malcolm arrived outside Enchanted Endings. He cut a tall, spindly figure, the type of middle-aged man people expected to be a funeral director, but he was a collector of antiquities by day and a considerable lush by night. Having inherited his parents' oil money in the 80s after their private plane crashed over the Sandias, he spent a considerable amount of time abroad procuring costly, unusual items for his collection of occult/religious antiquities. The Seal of Solomon was one of two antiquities he never expected to come across, the other being the infamous Holy Grail. His palms sweated as he grabbed the well-worn brass handle and pulled. A tiny bell tinkled overhead.

"In the back. Lock the door behind you, please."

Malcolm locked the deadbolt and skipped with a child's delight for a few seconds before catching himself and walking in his usual, slow stride. He straightened his bowtie and checked his watch. It was nearly nine o'clock. All Saints Day was in a few days and trick-or-treat was on Sunday at four o'clock.

"Malcolm, so nice to see you." McKay grinned and shifted in his chair. "Do sit down."

"Is this it?" Malcolm's otherworldly blue eyes sparked with excitement. He licked his lips like a hungry cat, barely containing his enthusiasm as he reached for the black velvet cloth with shaking hands. He withdrew a jeweler's loupe from his front suit pocket and leaned over the hardwood desk to inspect the lapis lazuli stone under the green banker's lamp.

"Well?"

"It's simply marvelous!" Malcolm looked up from the seal, which had a comforting weight to it. As he held it in his hand, his palm grew hotter and hotter until his skin felt scorched. He frowned. "What number are you thinking?"

McKay tore off a piece of paper from the old-fashioned message pad beside the rotary phone and scrawled a figure in black ink, sliding the paper across the desk to Malcolm.

"I'll have my accountant wire the money to you tomorrow morning. What time do you open?"

"Nine o'clock. We're closed Sundays." McKay beamed, pulling a bottle of Glenfiddich and brandy glasses from another desk drawer. "Shall we drink on it, then?"

"Yes," Malcolm nodded, salivating as he watched McKay pour the fine scotch.

***

While Malcolm and McKay sipped on their celebratory scotch, outside a woman in a dark purple cloak hovered in the shadows. "Is it here?"

"Yes, madam."

"You're positive?" It was very important for her to locate the Seal of Solomon so it didn't fall into the hands of the wrong individual. The biblical story was not a myth. Indeed, the stone could control demons and the dead and bring about the "End of Days."

The little girl ghost shook her head up and down twice, her long, silky pigtails bobbing. "I'm positive. Can I go now? I'm tired."

The little girl's image began to fade, but the woman in purple would not let her leave. "Stay with me a moment longer. I need you to describe what I am looking for, Penelope."

The little ghost girl sighed and nodded, pressing her lips together. Sometimes it was very trying being Stella's guide, but she had no choice in the matter. She was trapped here until she fulfilled her purpose, and as Stella explained, this was to help save humanity. Penelope had not found humanity kind enough to be saved. She was killed by a strange man while sleeping in her own bed; but then, Stella did seem to be the gentle grandmother she always wanted, baking sweets so the house smelled delicious all the time. Even though Penelope couldn't taste them anymore, she loved the way gingersnaps smelled so spicy and sweet. And she loved how the older woman took in all the strays in the neighborhood, even nursing that crow with the injured wing until he was able to fly. And she dearly loved Stella's granddaughter, Anne, though Anne wasn't even aware of her existence. Sadly, Anne didn't believe in the afterlife, something Stella was trying to rectify, since Anne came to live with her last year after her parents' tragic demise.

"Focus, Penelope."

"Yes, madam."

"And quit calling me 'madam.' Why, you'd think I was older than fifty-five, the way you carry on, I'll be knitting sweaters for cats and in my grave by the time I'm sixty."

Penelope smiled as she passed through the door of Enchanted Endings. She followed the sound of the men's voices and paused beside the desk to study the lapis lazuli carving.

McKay shivered. "Is it a bit cold in here?"

"I'm fine," Malcolm said. "I'll see my assistant wires you the money you requested as soon as possible and I will come back to collect my prize."

"Yes, I look forward to hearing from your assistant." Malcolm shivered then too as McKay showed him to the front door.

"He's coming," Penelope warned, startling Stella outside.

"Oh my," Stella cried and stepped farther back into the shadows beside the pharmacy as she watched Malcolm leave.

***

Ethel bent over the sink, watching the blood splash from her pen. She unscrewed her fountain pen and checked the ink cartridge, holding it up to the light. The cartridge contained what looked like blood. How was this even possible?

From the embalming room came a rustling. *The wind certainly has picked up, hasn't it?* Ethel thought to herself. She left her fountain pen in the bathroom sink, not wanting to stain her cashmere sweater, and turned to leave.

"Oh, my God! What—" Ethel's voice was cut off as Maeve Bellweather's corpse staggered toward her, her two saggy breasts swinging like pendulums, gnashing her teeth. Maeve's flesh spewed a stream of red and pink over the white subway tile walls. The hallway stank of formaldehyde.

Ethel managed to dodge the corpse's attack, retreating through the doorway into the darkened hallway leading back to the embalming room. Until now, Ethel had never feared the dark, but she found herself wishing she'd turned on the lights before heading to the ladies' room. She pressed her back against the tiled wall and inched her way toward the embalming room.

In the doorway, Mr. Chandler swayed back and forth. Sensing movement to his right, he turned his head and grinned sightlessly, his eyelids still superglued shut. The thread Ethel used to sew Mr. Chandler's mouth shut ripped open. The overpowering stink of formaldehyde assaulted Ethel as she screamed and dashed past the late Mr. Chandler, who swiveled and bobbled like a windup toy in her direction. Always a quick learner, he soon got his legs under control and charged. She picked up her metal makeup case and swung it at Mr. Chandler's face and did not stop swinging until Mr. Chandler lay on the floor, a pink mushy soup of brain leaking from his head like raw hamburger. Hot vomit raced up her throat, splashing over her feet as she struggled to breathe. Maeve had left the embalming room and now advanced from the hallway.

Ethel screamed as loud as she could, her eyes darting around for a better weapon. She pressed her back against the row of stainless steel drawers: a fatal mistake, for as she did so, the corpse of a young athlete kicked open the door to one of the drawers and crouched behind her. It sank its teeth into Ethel's jugular and pulled away a piece of her flesh, through to the carotid artery, which jiggled like a chicken breast, pumping in strong bursts until slowing with her dying heartbeat. The corpse gorged deep into her neck until it tore free her trachea. It dangled from its mouth like a gristly pink worm. It released Ethel's shoulders, and her body crumpled to the floor in a sticky sea of crimson billowing out from the bank of stainless steel doors.

***

Anne ran screaming towards her grandmother's house on Lake Drive, wielding her club like a wild Neanderthal as she approached a young man walking his dog. "Run! Run!" she shrieked, with a look of utter panic in her eyes.

The dog beside the young man sat upright, shivering, with its ears at attention. It lost control of its bladder as a sea of rats swarmed up from the sewer. One rat sank its yellow teeth into the scruff of its neck, and the dog was overtaken by the horde. The young man screamed as a rat sank its teeth into his Achilles tendon. He lost control of his bladder too as he saw what was coming up the hill, a mob of skeletons and decaying corpses, rotten and slimy, riddled with worms and beetles and other insects. He turned to flee. As one skeleton snatched at his wrist, another bit into his cheek and tore off a huge chunk, exposing his mandible. Another skeleton raked open his stomach with a talonlike fingernail and a foot of his intestine popped steaming from his belly. Anne didn't stop to help him as she fled.

Anne reached her grandmother's home just as Stella pulled up in her green Jetta, blaring Hungarian Roma music. Her face paled as she laid eyes on Anne and rushed out of her car, her cloak flapping in the wind behind her. "Anne, what's wrong?"

"They're coming." Anne's fair skin was flushed from running.

"Who?"

"The dead."

Without a word, Stella ushered Anne into the warm safety of her home. She laid her cloak on the front hall table and marched to the kitchen. "Come with me," she said, her usual gentle demeanor replaced with a brusque, businesslike approach, calm but commanding. "Penelope." The little girl ghost appeared in the kitchen beside the island of butcher block in the middle of the room. "Please check the yard and tell me what is going on."

Anne gasped as she watched the ghost of the little girl float past her and felt the air stir in her presence. "She's real." All her life she hadn't believed her grandmother's actions were more than playing with herbs in her kitchen or praying to a nonexistent goddess, futile acts, but they brought her grandmother happiness, so she let it be. And now she had seen a ghost. Did this mean her parents were ghosts? Was there an afterlife? Had Anne's spell worked simply because she was a witch descendant of a witch, descendant of another witch and so on? Could she do magick? The possibilities made her sway.

"Yes, girl, she's as real as you and me. Stay on your feet and focus, Anne. We have work to do. Obviously you've been doing something you shouldn't have, because your senses are awakened. This means you must have opened the door to the spirit world—and this close to All Saints Day, too. What a foolish thing you have done! Tell me everything as I work. Quickly! You're going to have to help me or you and I will both be dead before dawn." Stella grabbed multiple amber-colored jars from her arsenal in the cupboard, setting them down firmly on the counter one by one. "What did you do?"

"I was with Jimmy."

Stella's lips pursed. "You don't even need to say another word. That boy is bad news, but continue." She unscrewed one jar and drew a copper pot from beneath the butcher block.

"We were at the lake. At Mary Nohl's house."

"The Witch's House. Mmmmhmmm." Stella nodded, her silver bob shining.

"Jimmy found a ritual to call back Mary. We wanted to see if it would work."

"Foolish girl! You wanted to see if it would work?!" She slammed the flat of her hand against the butcher block. "You don't even know the strength of the powers you are messing with. The world of the dead is as real as the world of the living! On the dark side of the veil creatures exist you can't even begin to fathom. And you dared to be so arrogant as to call up the soul of that poor woman who was persecuted all her life as a witch?"

Anne's eyes filled with tears. She leaned against the butcher block, sobbing.

"Quit your whining and open these." Stella shoved multiple jars in Anne's direction and they flew across the polished countertop, almost crashing to the floor before Anne caught them. She hurried to open them all.

"Did you use a pentagram?"

"Y-yes."

"And black candles?"

"Y-yes, grandmother."

"Foolish girl," Stella muttered, continuing to work.

"What are we doing?"

"First, we are going to create a spell to protect the perimeter of this house from the dead. And then we are going to go after the seal. If we are lucky enough to get the seal, we will close the portal to hell. By opening up this portal, you have unleashed hell on earth. One of the seven gates is unlocked. The dead now walk the earth. It is the End of Days."

"How is this going to help?"

"You've never been one to trust your grandmother's magick, have you? Just like your mother." Stella grinned. She picked up the first jar and measured out a few teaspoons full. "Agrimony—Shielding and hex-breaking, aids sleep, brings luck towards you and is powerful in spell reversal. Element air. Angelica—Also called Archangel. It is a very powerful protection herb, healing, creates harmony and courage and helps in exorcisms. Aids vision. Element air. Ash—Spells relating to the sea, protection, and luck. Make your Yule log from ash and burn to bring prosperity. Yggdrasil was an Ash tree. Element water. Bergamot—Money, prosperity and sleep. Protects from both evil and illness. Good for luck and wealth. Increases magical power. Element fire. Birch—Protection, exorcism and purification. Dispels lightning, infertility, and the evil eye. Associated with Yule. Element water. Black Pepper—Banishing negativity, exorcism, and offers protection and help with inner strength. Element fire. Horehound—Protective against evil doings. Helps with mental clarity during ritual; stimulates creativity/inspiration; balances personal energies and healing. Element earth. Thyme—for fairy magic. Bay—protection from evil spirits.

"Rosemary to ward off nightmares, for divination, and healing." She picked up another jar and measured another few teaspoons full. "Rose from the garden. Planted to attract fairies. It grows best when stolen. The petals sprinkled around the house calm stress and household upheavals." She continued to explain as she measured from each jar, a strong, comforting floral steam rising to the ceiling. "Raspberry—the brambles used to be hung above doorways and windows to offer protection. It was also done at death so a loved one wouldn't return to their home after burial. Cinnamon—the leaves of the tree were made into wreaths and used to decorate ancient temples. When burned as incense, it aids in healing and protection. Mint—for prosperity and love. Basil—to reduce stress, for warmth, and for abundance. Clove—for protection, banishing unwanted spirits, and relieving strife. And lastly, ginger—to assure success and motivation and usher in love. Add a little sea salt to help cleanse your property of negative entities and spells, and you are golden." She winked at Anne as she closed her eyes in prayer and said a few words above the steaming concoction. She took the copper pot off the burner when she finished. "Now we wait for that to cool a bit. Go into the walk-in pantry and bring out the three milk jugs sitting on the left."

"Can I ask you something first?"

"If you must, but time is of the essence. The longer we wait to fix things, the worse they will be."

Anne blinked and gave her grandmother a sheepish grin. She couldn't believe she was even asking this, but she had to know the answer. "If witches are real, are vampires and werewolves real too?" Surely, her grandmother would know. She closed her eyes and focused on her breathing because she felt her chest tightening like iron binding her ribcage.

"That's a story for another time."

"Wait—they're real!?"

"Anne." Her grandmother sighed. "Focus on the task at hand."

Anne nodded and brought her grandmother the three jugs. "This looks like tap water."

"It's not."

"What is it, then?"

"Go back in the pantry and grab the plastic bag from the top shelf."

She did and when she returned she said, "Grandma, these are super soakers. We're going to fight the "End of Days" with plastic guns?"

"And holy water and a little arm muscle. I'm a witch, but I'm pagan, not Wiccan, girl. Your grandma still goes to church on Sunday." Her grandmother nodded, her lips pursed, as she opened a gallon jug. "Start filling."

When they had filled all four guns, two for each of them slung over their shoulders by the straps, Stella selected a meat cleaver from the knife block on the counter. Its blade flashed a threatening grin as she wielded it in her right hand. "Pick your weapon, girl. We're going into combat."

Anne gaped like a fish out of water. "Are you serious? Grandma, this isn't a made for T.V. movie. Shouldn't we call for help?"

Stella sighed. "Anne, do I really have to answer that question?" She turned to look out her kitchen window as a group of the dead came around the bend in her drive. They were a motley crew moving faster than she anticipated for a bunch of—skeleton cows? She blinked and laughed.

Yes, those were steers coming up the drive, gnashing their teeth, tossing their heads, and stamping their hooves, ready to charge.

"Before we go, we're going to draw a cross above every door and every window on each floor of the house. Pour some of my spell into another bowl and get going on the second floor. Work clockwise from east to west, girl."

When they were done, they met back in the kitchen.

"On my count, I'm going to open the kitchen side door. Run as fast as you can to the car and start it."

"What about you?"

"I'll be right behind you."

"You expect me to outrun cattle?"

"It's only a couple hundred yards, girl. You were on the track team, weren't you?" Stella shook her head and laughed.

"Okay. One, two, three," Stella cried as the door to the night flew open. A great gust of wind blew in a cyclone of leaves and the cattle bellowed their supernatural bellows, even though they lacked flesh. Anne dashed towards the car. "Shoot anything you can," Stella yelled, "and slash the rest to hell, girl!" She ran out the kitchen door, aiming for the first steer with the super soaker.

A few seconds later, they were both in the car, breathless. Anne shook. She peered out into the darkness held back by the lamplight on either side of the drive for a few hundred feet, but beyond was a black so thick and inky, she couldn't see Satan, even if he existed.

"Drive," Stella said as she slapped the dash with her hand and glared back at the rest of the group of cattle charging up the drive, followed by a crowd of decomposing corpses, some freshly dead and some further along in stages of decomposition, their clothes wet with biological juices, hanging in tatters, maggots cascading from their mouths and eye sockets. One corpse limped along with its left foot turned backwards, a nasty compound break not doing much to slow it down.

"Where are we going?" Anne gritted her teeth as she plowed through the remaining cattle and an army of the dead with her grandmother's green Jetta.

"To Malcolm's house. Turn left at the end of the drive and step on the gas. Mow down anything you see." Stella held on to the grab handle, or the "oh, fuck me bar," as she called it.

The ghost girl, Penelope, popped up in the back seat, flickering in and out of existence on this plane. "We have to hurry to Malcolm's house. Something is wrong."

"Can she *not* do that?" Anne glanced at her grandmother.

"Do what?" Penelope rested her elbows on the headrests of the front seats.

"Just show up whenever you want. Do you have to scare a person half to death?" Anne glowered at Penelope.

"I'm sorry. Am I interfering with your being *alive*?" Penelope chuckled at Anne and stuck out her tongue with her eyes crossed.

"Girls." Stella shook her head. "Try to get along. Now is not the time for a feud."

***

"The Flight of the Bumblebee" by Nikolai Rimsky-Korsakov boomed as Malcolm sat sipping a brandy beside the fireplace in his study, his pale, waxy complexion softened by the light of multiple candles. He grinned, holding the Seal of Solomon in his right hand. Malcolm felt the lapis lazuli warm in his hand. It stirred like a cat waking from a nap, or was that his imagination? He surely did not believe in things that go bump in the night or the "End of Days." The world was more likely to end in nuclear war than the opening of the seven gates of hell. Hell was humanity and what it inflicted upon itself and other animals. There was no such thing as witches. There was no such thing as the devil, and there surely was no such thing as God, as Malcolm learned long ago, when his childhood prayers weren't answered.

He opened his palm. The veins of gold in the lapis lazuli flashed like lightning. He ran his thumb over the carving, luxuriating in the feel of the indentations massaging his thumb pad.

Darkness pressed in against his home, along with the bare limbs of the elms. The wind picked up off the lake. He had just nodded off when a great splintering of glass startled him awake. The menacing shards glittered like gems by the light of the fire. He set his brandy snifter down and put the Seal of Solomon in the pocket of his smoking jacket as he backed away from the window with his arms shielding his face.

A barred owl shrieked at Malcolm and beat its powerful wings in fury and confusion. With an almost four-foot wingspan, the owl was a formidable opponent to the pampered Malcolm. The diameter of its talons was about three inches, talons it could use to capture other birds, reptiles, and even amphibians, if the opportunity presented itself. At the moment, it dug its talons into the fleshy palm of Malcolm's left hand, pecking and tearing with its sharp beak, its pale, creamy underside glowing rose by the firelight. Its cries chilled Malcolm's blood, which now ran in great rivulets from his hand down his wrists and into the arms of his smoking jacket. He crumpled in a pile of burgundy fabric, sobbing and whimpering, pleading with the owl, "Stop, oh God, please stop! For the love of God, please stop!" His cries faded. A juicy tearing sound filled the room as the music ended and the record player crackled. The owl lifted its head and swallowed Malcolm's eyelids like small fish as it shifted its weight on Malcolm's face and bent down to feast on his fatty jowls, ruby speckles of blood dotting its grey-barred chest.

***

Mary Louise Nohl arrived outside her home about two hours after rising from her grave. She stood in front of the barbed wire-topped fence, one foot now shoeless with only the top of her sock surviving. It flapped like a giant tongue every time she moved. Pebbles and glass ground deep into her heel, but she felt nothing. The embalming fluid Ethel used to replace her blood stained her green dress a darker shade of the forest and her red brick sweater a deeper maroon in splotches. She no longer had the artificial rosy glow of the living. Her skin was ash and bone colored. Wire jutted from her lips, curling up and out like whiskers or strange wriggling worms. Her eyes were milky; she was blind. She stank of earth and formaldehyde. A dry rasping rose from her throat as she swayed, staring sightless at the red pulsing rays of light rotating from the grate of the storm sewer. The waves shone an eerie crimson as they crashed to shore, droplets glinting like garnets.

A clowder of alley cats, scraggly, ears ragged, coats dingy with dirt, and hunger lurking in their slit eyes sat in a circle in the front yard before the cement fish wearing a hat; it perched upright like a person, its tailfin pointing towards the earth, its one blue glass eye shimmering like light playing over the lake. The pack of coyotes had since departed to other hunting grounds.

A mourning dove stirred and cried a nervous volley of cooing. The yellow eyes of a few raccoons glowed from the trees. All the animals of the night had awakened to bear witness to the end of the world.

***

Alicia found it odd Ethel hadn't picked up the phone, but after an exhausting day of gardening, she didn't want to hike over to the family funeral home. She assumed Ethel had probably gotten a last-minute call before leaving work. She took her sister's plate of meatloaf out of the oven; it had long since dried out. Just as she scraped the meatloaf and mashed potatoes into the garbage can, the front doorbell rang. Alicia glanced at her watch. Who could be calling so late? She drew her pink terry housecoat closer to her slender frame and trudged to the front door in her matching slippers. She wrinkled her nose as she approached the door. What was that smell? It smelled like rotting meat.

"Hello," she said. She waited a minute. No one answered. She opened the door. There was nobody there. She crept out onto the front porch and peered out beyond the cedars flanking the steps, which was the last mistake she ever made.

Blood stained Ethel's powder blue cashmere sweater. She staggered toward her sister, her arms outstretched as if to hug her. A six-foot-four corpse dressed in a grey pinstripe suit lunged from the shadows and sank its sharp incisors into Alicia's wrist, tearing away in savage haste. Hot blood spurted from Alicia's veins, staining the corpse's teeth a frothy red as it continued to chomp down on her arm with gusto.

Alicia screamed like a rabbit dying, the unearthly shriek halting abruptly as she was overcome by two more corpses. The last thing Alicia saw before her eyes closed was the gold of her sister's cross as Ethel knelt over her.

The neighbors woke next door. Startled from their slumber, lights flicked on up and down the block as more than one household reached for their cell phones to dial 911.

Something was terribly wrong.

***

Anne, shaking, pulled up in Malcolm's driveway. Stella sat silent beside her; the hood of her purple cloak hid her face. "I have to go inside," Stella said. "You can come with me or stay here. The choice is yours, but be quick about it. Every second another life could be taken counts."

Anne swallowed and gripped the steering wheel like a drowning woman gripped a life preserver. "I'll come with you." She chewed on a hangnail, ripping it off and causing herself to bleed.

"You're sure." Stella turned to look at Anne.

The click of her seatbelt being undone was the only answer Stella needed. She leapt from the car with a catlike grace, brandishing her meat cleaver in her right hand, grasping the straps of her super soakers with her left. "Try to save the holy water. Only use it if you must. Use your knife first." Stella rushed to the front door, breathing a sigh of relief when no corpses popped out of the shadows.

"Malcolm is dead. The stone is here, though." Penelope reappeared beside them as they crouched on the front porch behind the evergreen hedge.

"Will you quit sneaking up on us?" Anne glared.

"Only if you promise to quit breathing." Penelope grinned, shaking her glossy blonde pigtails. The smile looked unnatural on her sullen, pinched face.

"Girls!" Stella glanced around before picking up a rock from underneath the hedge. She slammed it into the front bay window and cleared out the remaining sharp pieces of glass from the windowpane with one arm shielded in her purple cloak. With ease, she slipped through the dark hole into the house. Candlelight flickered off to the left in a wood paneled room.

"This comes to you so naturally, grandmother. You'd think you were an accomplished cat burglar or something." Anne followed behind Stella with Penelope floating to their right. "Can't you pretend to walk?"

"And ruin my ghostly fabulousness?" Penelope quipped. "Not a chance." She floated right in front of Anne's face, tickling her nose with the wide ribbon cinched around the waist of her old-fashioned dress.

"Stop it."

"Both of you stop it." Stella stepped through the doorway into chaos. Glass littered the floor. White and grey feathers sifted down on a warm updraft of air. Bloody footprints led out of the room through the other doorway to the right. "Locate the stone and let's roll. No pun intended."

Together, Stella and Anne scanned the desk and the bookcases while Penelope floated around the perimeter of the room. "It's right here," Penelope called. Underneath the side table containing an empty brandy snifter gleamed a cobalt blue stone with gold veins.

"Got it. Let's go." The three left the room and headed back towards the car.

***

"Where are we going?" Anne looked to her grandmother for guidance as they turned out of Malcolm's driveway. Stella clutched the lapis lazuli carving, afraid to let go. She sat with her eyes closed.

"She's concentrating." Penelope leaned over from the back seat.

"Concentrating on what?"

"On trying not to kill either of you," Stella answered as she opened her eyes and took a very deep breath. "I was trying to sense if Mary was out there."

"What difference would that make, grandma?"

"Mary is the beacon calling to the dead. The portal to hell opened up at her home after you performed the spell to call her back from the dead."

"You did what?" Penelope smirked.

"Shut up, ghost girl." Anne bit her lip to keep from cursing in her grandmother's presence.

"We have to reverse the spell. The only way to do that is to command Mary to go back to her slumber, and then we can close the gate."

"How are we going to do that?"

"I'm going to control her body. It's like a vehicle. I can drive it with this stone, but I have to remember the correct spell. It's been decades since I studied any necromancy." Stella frowned, deep wrinkles carving into her smooth brow.

"How can I help?" Anne kept driving onward because she didn't know what else to do.

"Pull over to the side of the road and turn on the overhead light. Keep the headlights on and watch for any sign of movement. Run over anything that comes our way. And Penelope, I'm sending you ahead to scope out Mary Nohl's house. I need to know how many of the dead are waiting and where they are posted. They'll be watching for Mary's arrival, if she's not already there."

"Okay." Penelope passed through the back car door without any hesitation.

"That is so freaky. I don't know how you stand it." Anne shook her head.

"You get used to it. Now let me work, child." Stella drew a black tome from the folds of her cloak. Anne switched on the overhead light. Fifteen minutes passed before Stella spoke again. "Drive to the Witch's House."

The two woman drove in silence through the night. Beach Drive curved like a serpent to the east of them as they wound their way toward the shore of Lake Michigan and "The Witch's House." The hairs on Anne's arms and the back of her neck rose stiff, alerting her to mortal danger. Her heart pounded louder than a snare drum as she drove the final hundred feet and saw the spectacle spread out before them.

The animals of the forest gathered in the front sculpture garden. Raccoons, skunk, possums, cats, dogs, and coyotes commingled. Some perching on the giant heads rising from the ground, others sitting beside sculptures of animals and children playing. Deer froze in place. Owls watched from the roof of the cottage. Anne rolled down her window. She could hear the lake beating against the rocks. Beating and beating. It almost lulled her to sleep. She struggled to keep her eyes open.

"Anne." Stella jostled her shoulder. "Anne."

"Hmm?" Anne struggled to keep her eyes open. It would be so nice to sleep. Just to go to sleep. To dream. To wake up and be somewhere else.

"Anne!" Stella shook her more forcefully. "Damn it!" Stella jumped out of the car and slammed the door behind her. She left her granddaughter in the driver's seat on watch. Stella held her meat cleaver in front of her for protection as she advanced slowly to the fence. Beyond the garden, she saw the red light, the gateway to hell, pulsing in time with the beat of her own heart. An endless line of corpses backlit with the red light, emerged from the sewer and climbed up the steep embankment from the breakwater below.

Anne sat upright in her seat at the jarring slam of the car door. She got out of the car and shouldered her super soakers, aiming for the first corpse she saw, feeling rather foolish. Was this really happening? It felt like something out of a bad Stephen King movie. But no, she hit the first corpse in the chest with the holy water and watched in surprise as steam rose from the body of an elderly man who caught fire. His body fell to the ground, twisting and curling in upon itself in a fetal position as it turned into a pile of embers and ash. Tiny sparks floated upwards into the night.

Anne shot a steady stream of water again and again as she watched her grandmother kneel on the blacktop in front of the driveway where Anne and Jimmy had summoned Mary Nohl. Her grandmother raised her arms, the meat cleaver pointed upward toward the heavens as she chanted something softly. The ground shook. A lone coyote howled. And the ground shook. A cat hissed. And the ground shook. An owl hooted. And the ground shook. Mary Nohl cried out. And the ground shook.

"Mary." Stella turned towards Mary's corpse. "Come to me, Mary."

Mary walked toward Stella with her arms outstretched like a toddler's. Anne was busy shooting streams of water at the onslaught of corpses stumbling up the embankment. A raccoon bared its teeth and charged her ankle, diverting her attention. The animals were in a frenzy because of the danger from the zombies, afraid for their own lives. Anne knelt and slashed at the critter with her knife. A jagged red line appeared on its whiskered snout. It hissed and raised a paw to swipe at her calf. Anne cried out and fell to the ground in surprise and because she hated raccoons with their creepy masks, dropping her super soakers and the knife. The metal clang startled the raccoon and it bolted for the safety of the pines across the street, but the coyotes were hungry, so hungry. They advanced as one with powerful strides upon the girl sprawled on the pavement before them.

"Anne!" Stella rushed to save her granddaughter, but was overpowered by the animals. One of the coyotes lunged at her right leg and wrestled her to the ground. She kicked at its head to no avail as it dug its teeth deeper into her leg. "Anne! Take the stone!" Stella tossed the lapis lazuli carving to her granddaughter who caught it awkwardly between her armpit and side.

"Grandmother," Anne cried. She tried to run to Stella's side, but a huge alpha male that stood as tall as her waist blocked her path.

Anne watched her grandmother slash at the coyotes encircling her. She was able to keep them at bay for a moment. "The spell you used earlier. Say it again."

"But—"

"Say it, Anne, just say it. Hold the stone up above your head and say the words backwards to reverse the spell. I'll help you, repeat after me." Her grandmother spoke the words.

Anne held the stone high overhead. It throbbed with heat. "*Ihim taif tou lov coh da ieD oilixua te muut reti tiuuN out omina muc irigral I mutcejbo coh odnehearped mumitlu munu ie ad tnrueisnart aaropmet sujuc suoutrom.*"

A single bolt of lightning cracked and the thunder boomed and the ground shook. Penelope appeared crying beside Stella as she watched the coyotes eat her.

Mary Nohl turned and lifted her head in Anne's direction. She pulled her mouth into a rictus, the wires wiggling about her lips as she shuffled toward the waves beating against the shoreline. The red square of light blinked off and then on once more as Mary's pale skin glowed pink. And then she faded. A loud sonic boom stung Anne's eardrums as all the remaining corpses combusted and fell to ashes, sparks dancing on the wind. Tears streamed over Anne's face. Her grandmother lay surrounded by coyotes with bloody snouts, dead. She had sacrificed herself for her granddaughter. The dead were gone and only the living remained.

HOW ROMEO AND MORI SAVED THE WORLD

"Without stories we would not exist."—Romeo the Ant

"Boss, really?! The world is about to end, and you stuck me with the new guy?" Romeo's antennae bobbed up and down as he shifted his little ant feet.

"Where? Where's the new guy?" The raven's head swiveled back and forth like an animatronic.

"You, bird brain. You're the new guy." Romeo hopped up and down.

"No, I'm Mori. Nice to meet you." The raven stared down at the purple ant circling him.

"What happened to your feet?"

"Oh, no! Did they get chopped off again?"

"No, you big feather duster. You've got a biped's feet with five toes!"

"They work just fine." Mori danced a little jig.

"This is ridiculous. I can't work under these conditions. I'm requesting an immediate transfer to the Beta Quadrant of The Milky Way Galaxy. *Immediately*." Romeo hopped up on the consul interface and started jumping on random buttons. "And I need a mocha caramel Frappuccino for one Hormiga Formīca with two extra pumps of caramel. Not car-uh-mel. The second "a" is silent. Hello?" Romeo pounced on the intercom conference button, watching the blank liquid crystal monitor. "Did you get my order? And could somebody pulleez put some socks on Tweety's feet? His toes are creeping me out."

"Oh, you think this is creepy? You should meet pigeon Peg Leg Steve. An unfortunate forestry service accident ended my previous career, but the big cheese was able to hook me up with these cyber enhanced human feet. Watch this. I'm the baddest Intergalactic Federation Librarian in the galaxy." Mori shot up two feet taller. He was eye to eye with Romeo and tilted his head, watching Romeo pacing the control consul.

"Don't even think about it, you oversized feather boa. I heard your stomach growling. Even though I am a cyber engineered ant, I'm equipped with an unsavory toxin to discourage predators from eating me.

I wouldn't agree with you." Romeo drew himself up to his full half inch in height and bared his mandibles at Mori.

"Got it. Don't eat your coworker. Rule *numero uno*."

A bunch of wavy lines coalesced into an image on the spaceship's consul display. "Good evening, gentlemen. Colonel Muenster here," the big wedge of cheese greeted them in a gruff voice. The Colonel's only distinguishing features were a pair of bushy brown eyebrows, one perpetually raised higher than the other, giving him a permanent quizzical look. He had no mouth, one of the galaxy's many mysteries, because he was in charge of the Intergalactic Federation of Traveling Librarians. Nobody knew how a wedge of cheese had achieved this prestigious position.

"Colonel? I thought you were Commander Muenster." Romeo stared at the screen.

"I was promoted during the War of Cheese in 2025." Colonel Muenster cleared his throat and raised his left eyebrow a tad higher. "Anything else before I give you two your new assignment?"

"Nope. I'm good." Mori shifted his feet.

"Did you get my drink order?"

"No." Colonel Muenster shifted on screen, looming in closer to Romeo.

"How's an ant supposed to work under these conditions? I need sugar!" Romeo feigned a dramatic faint; opening one eye, he saw no one paid him any mind, so he remained lying on his side.

"As part of the Intergalactic Federation of Librarians, it is your duty to travel the Milky Way to dispense and collect information and clear library fines for the posterity of the Galaxy. It has come to my attention that the New USSR has set Earth's Story Tree on fire in an attempt to erase humanity's history and turn Earth into a war machine."

"The Story Tree is on fire! Oh no!" Romeo dropped his head.

"Yes. It's been burning for three days and three nights and is almost completely destroyed. If The New USSR succeeds in their mission, Earth, whose Story Tree roots cradle the planet in its nest, will die, becoming a dead ball of clay, and The New USSR will ramp up production of their war machines to conquer other planets and soon other galaxies. People's souls will die without stories to nourish them. Humanity will forget where it came from. We've got to think of something and fast. I just received word because our link was broken."

"How sad." Mori wiped a tear from his eye with a wingtip.

"But all is not lost, gentlemen. Romeo, I am sending you and Mori to Earth with a librarian's bag to gather all the stories you can to bring to Story Woman, the caretaker of the Story Tree. Everyone's story, no matter how small and unimportant it may seem, is needed to revive the roots of the tree and foster new growth, so be vigilant and make sure you talk to as many people as you can. Is this understood?"

"Yes, sir!" Mori saluted Colonel Muenster on screen.

"You will find the librarian's bag on board your ship. You leave immediately."

"Thank you, Colonel Muenster." Romeo marched to the gateway. "Hurry up, bird brain. We have a time-sensitive mission."

Mori walked to the gateway as a large clear vacuum tube lowered over them. A muffled Mori squawked, "Oh, I hate traveling by vacuum tube. My feathers will take at least a week to groom after this. Sigh."

Before Romeo could reply, the two were sucked into the interplanetary vacuum system and spat out in a cloud of loose black feathers and red dust from the mesas of New Mexico. An ancient leather satchel followed, nearly crushing Romeo.

Romeo shook his foot at the vacuum transponder control bot as it flew up through the clouds. "You cock-a-ninny. Watch where you go tossing things!"

But with the roar of the vacuum, all Mori heard was, "Wah. Wah-wah-wah-wah. WAH! WAH!" Mori picked up the librarian bag up and adjusted the strap with his beak. It was almost as big as he was, so he used his cyber feet to adjust himself to the proper carrying height. They'd landed near a xeriscape parking lot beside a grocery.

"Where are we?" Mori's head darted towards a bunch of fast food fries abandoned beside a dusty Kia. A roadrunner eyed the raven, its beak stuffed with fries. "I'm so hungry." Mori waddled and creaked on his cyber enhanced feet. "There are so many people."

"Quit gawking like a dodo. They can't see us until we speak to them. The librarian bag has a special cloaking mechanism. Just don't get stomped on." Romeo put his head to the hot blacktop, following a yummy scent trail to an old woman's green hatch chilé cart outside the grocery; the aroma of roasting chilés overwhelmed him.

"Let's go talk to that little girl on the mechanical horse." Mori nodded towards the small girl riding the sun faded painted pony.

"Hi." The little girl smiled at Mori and Romeo. She liked bugs and was always on the lookout for them.

"Wait, you can see us?" Romeo gawked at her.

"Why does your bird friend have funny feet?"

"I've asked the same question myself. I'm Romeo and this is Mori."

"What's wrong with my feet?"

"Focus, bird brain. Nobody really cares about your feet, okay?"

"I'm Sara. Why are you purple?"

"Well… because… huh. Nobody's ever asked me that before. I don't know." For once in his life, Romeo was stumped.

"It's okay. I'm only four and I don't know everything."

"Well, Sara. It just so happens that Mori and I are traveling librarians collecting stories to save Earth's Story Tree. Do you have a story you can tell us?"

"No." She shook her head.

"Aw, everyone's got a story to tell." Mori hiked himself up on his cyber feet, so he was eye level with Sara.

"People need stories, Sara. Without them, they wouldn't remember who they were or where they came from. You see, if you ever forget who you are and what's important, you simply turn to the first page of your favorite story and begin again." Romeo's antennae quivered as he did a little jig of satisfaction, which made Sara giggle.

"What's in the bag?"

"Are we supposed to tell Earthers what's in the bag, Romeo?"

"Will you kindly not breathe on me and could you pick me up—Hey! What are you doing? Put me down!"

Romeo dangled from Mori's beak, his tiny legs running in the air before he was placed on Mori's shoulder. Romeo stomped his feet.

"Ow! Will. You. Quit. Hurting. Me."

"I was just in your mouth. It smells like garlic. Uck! What have you been eating? Maybe next time you could just pick me up in a box with your beak? It would be more dignified." Romeo huffed, opening and closing his mandibles.

"Sorry. Anyhoo, are we supposed to tell her about the bag?"

"That bag?" Sara pointed.

"I thought you said she couldn't see the bag?" Mori tilted his head towards Romeo.

"Well, if she can see us, I guess she can." Romeo paused. "Sara, you are a remarkable little girl. I bet you have at least one story we can take back in our librarian bag."

"What does the Story Tree look like?" Sara stared at Romeo.

"Well, it's this gigantic tree that's so big, nobody on Earth has ever seen the top. In fact, most people don't even know it exists. Only very special people with a very special gift can see it. Its roots start at the bottom of the planet and it grows up through the center of the Earth. In fact, the roots form a nest that Earth rests inside. The trunk grows up above the grass and travels high into outer space where the tree's branches hug the stars. And its leaves are all the colors of the rainbow. Story Woman lives inside the tree and is the Keeper of the Stories."

"Like a head librarian?"

"Yes, just like that." Romeo nodded.

"Well, I do have one story. Mom says it's not nice to lie, but I swear I saw him when we were out on the mesa. He was playing his flute."

"Who did you see, Sara?"

"Kokopelli."

"Could you tell us the story of Kokopelli?"

"Yes."

"Okay. Hang on one second. I need to plug Romeo into the recorder in the librarian bag." Mori fished in the bag with his beak, trying not to topple Romeo from his shoulder.

"How do you plug in an ant?"

"Well, Romeo's a cyber ant, so he's like a robot and he can record things."

"This is so humiliating. I've asked them when they do updates on me to move the position of my—"

"And if I plug this USB plug into his butt like this..." Mori said as he fidgeted behind Romeo. He lifted a tiny hatch on the ant's backside and plugged him into the librarian bag.

"Ants don't have butts." Sara giggled.

"I guess you could say he's got a stick up his butt or he's got a..." Mori looked at Sara and silenced himself. "Never mind. You're too young for that joke." Mori chuckled. Romeo could no longer hear him in "record mode." His head bent down and his antennae pointed towards the heavens with narrow beams of green light projecting from his eyes.

"Now you can tell me the story of Kokopelli. Just talk to Romeo." The wind coming down the mesa ruffled Mori's already disheveled feathers and Sara's hair.

"One day Kokopelli found the Ant People living in the dark. Kokopelli helped the Ant People travel to the Red World of the Cat People and then up to the Yellow World filled with spiders. All this time, he played his flute and taught the Ant People to plant food and hunt. The Ant People dug a hole to the Blue World and traveled with Kokopelli to a place where he couldn't play his music. Water fell on them from the hole, but Spider Woman spun a web to keep them dry. Then the Ant People travelled with Kokopelli to the Green World and the Cloud Spirits shot Kokopelli with lightning. Kokopelli was able to play his flute again. The Cloud People created wings from his back skin and Kokopelli asked the Ant People to join the Cloud People in happiness and light. He taught the Ant People about Great Spirit who could lead them out of the darkness into the light. The end."

"Thank you, Sara." Mori unplugged Romeo and he sprang into motion.

"Did we get it? It's a good one?"

"We got it and it's a good one. The bag has more heft than before." Mori lifted it with his beak.

"Unlike your bird brain, I'm sure. Oh, my ants! That delicious smell!"

"Those are *abuela's* Hatch chilés."

"A Hatch chilé." Romeo's mandibles worked double time, his antennae pointed in the direction of the roasting chilés with the earthy aroma—very delectable. "Oh man, after all that work, my battery needs a sugar jump start. You know I convert food to sugar that runs my battery, right?" Romeo scurried to the cart and halted, his eyes glowing with the a burnt orange light as he was unplugged, indicating his batteries were run down.

A petite red ant sat atop a fallen chilé in the late afternoon sun.

"You delectable creature."

"Are you referring to me or the Hatch chilé?"

"Why, of course, you." Romeo sauntered over to her, his head to the ground, tracking her pheromones. Their antennae met. "What's your name?"

"Blossom."

"A saguaro blossom couldn't be sweeter."

"Laying it on a bit thick, aren't you, Shakespeare? Why do your eyes glow and why is your skin the color of dusk?"

"The color of dusk? He's purple," Mori cackled.

"Beat it, bird brain."

"Okay, lover boy, you've got five minutes until we're beamed on board the ship to travel to Earth's Story Tree. I've sent the signal."

"Blossom, how would you like to travel the stars with me?"

"With you?"

"And my bird friend here. We're intergalactic librarians traveling the galaxy and collecting stories. Earth's Story Tree was set on fire. The fire's been put out and now we're hoping if we feed it enough stories, it will regenerate with time and Earth will be saved."

"Sounds like a good mission." Blossom stared up at the sky.

"Hey, Mori, can you put that chilé in the librarian bag? I could use a good snack. And be careful not to put your beak all over it."

"Are you taking my story to the Story Tree now?" Sara squatted down beside Romeo.

"Yes. We're collecting them one by one to feed the tree."

"Sara, who are you talking to?" Sara turned to answer her *abuela* and when she glanced back by the cart, the librarians and their bag were gone.

"No one, *abuela.* I was just telling myself a story."

Meanwhile, the Library Federation Starship hovered in space before the injured Story Tree. Here and there traces of orange fire burned the blackened branches to ash. The Story Tree's once vibrant rainbow-colored leaves hung tattered and smudged a ghost grey.

"You ready, Romeo?"

"Let's do this, Mori." Romeo hopped up on the ship's consule so Mori could plug him into a port connected to a large antenna to beam the story of the Ant People across space.

Blossom stood close to Romeo, in awe at the beauty of the galaxy. Romeo's eyes glowed and his antennae pointed toward the Story Tree. Together, Mori and Blossom watched a tiny shoot sprout and flourish in a dazzling array of colors. Story Tree Woman appeared behind a veil of moonlight and sprinkled the Tree with a golden dusting of starlight. Mori nodded hello.

"Do you think the Story Tree will be all right?" Blossom asked.

"As long as people keep telling their stories, I think it will be, Blossom." Mori unplugged Romeo and he came to life again.

"Mori, could you get us that Hatch chilé? I'm starving and it's going to be a long journey back home." Together, Romeo and Blossom nibbled on the roasted pepper.

"I'm famished. I could really go for a piece of cheese."

Colonel Muenster popped up on the display. "I heard that."

"Sorry, sir." Mori fluffed his feathers and they all laughed as the Librarian Federation Starship sped through infinite time and space.

BURY HIM BY THE RIVER

The author has taken certain liberties with geographical locations.

Their trip renting an Airbnb in Louisville, Kentucky had gone from party to murder pretty quick.

Later that evening, they sat alone in their apartment, wondering if they had made the right decision. "Let's clean this place up, shower, and get on the road," Mitch said.

"Are you kidding me? We killed someone, Mitch. You think nobody's going to know it was us? Four out of state kids with fake IDs, college-bound in the fall, who rented a place for the weekend. Who do you think the authorities are going to come looking for?" Kaylie flopped back on the white couch, not even caring if they were getting their security deposit back for tracking in all the mud, blood, and leaves on the floor and furniture.

Margaret sat next to her, a crying ragdoll; her wavy red hair hid her face.

"Oh, will you stop it with the sniveling, Mags," Danny punched one of the decorative throw pillows.

"Well, I'm sorry, but we just left him there. We shouldn't have left him there." She wiped her nose with the back of her hand, shivering.

"We had to leave him there or we would have been found out. We can clean this mess up, shower, grab our things, and hit the road back to Wisconsin, all right?" Danny soothed Margaret by rubbing her back.

"Don't touch me!" Margaret jumped up from the couch. "I don't want to talk to any of you ever again."

"Mags, wait!" Mitch grabbed her by the arm.

"You're hurting me!" Margaret twisted her arm to get away.

"Get your hands off her!" Danny stood between his girlfriend and his best friend.

"I wasn't going to hurt her. You honestly think I would hurt Mags, Danny?"

"I don't know. You were pretty quick to do what you did."

"We *had* to do it. We had no fucking choice. He would have told. It's done. It's over with." Mitch threw his hands up in the air. "Everybody be cool. Let's clean this shit up, shower, grab our stuff and get on the road fast before they start looking for us. And not one of us is going to call the cops." He made eye contact with each one of them. "We've all got scholarships waiting for us back home and the rest of our lives ahead of us. This is just what my dad calls a 'little bump in the road.'"

"A little bump in the road?! Are you even listening to yourself, Mitch? You're fucking crazy." Margaret backed away from Mitch.

"You gonna get your bitch in line or am I going to need to give her an attitude adjustment, Danny? Cuz I am not"—he emphasized each word with a finger poking Danny in the chest—"going to prison for some Hicksville retard slaying. Just ain't my style, man. There are people I do things for and people I do things to, you get my drift?" Mitch nodded in Margaret's direction.

"Yeah, I got you," Danny put his arms around his girlfriend and whispered something in her ear before she broke free, sobbing, and ran for the room she shared with Kaylie. She'd been fighting with Danny and didn't agree with what happened that night. In fact, it was so awful, she wasn't sure she even wanted to see Danny when they got home.

"Kaylie, go check on Mags and make sure you've got her cell. We don't want any slip-ups." Mitch nodded to Danny. "You give me yours too, man. She's your girlfriend and you're a threat."

"What the fuck, Mitch," Danny threw his hands up in front of his face in a *come at me* gesture but straightened up. He and Mitch had been friends since kindergarten, and he knew when his friend wasn't joking around. He slid his cell from the back pocket of his jean shorts and Mitch palmed it as he walked away.

"We leave in an hour, after we clean up what we tracked in here and shower. Anybody not ready gets left behind," yelled Mitch, walking backwards down the hall toward his room.

***

The idea of going out Tuesday night away from Louisville had appealed to all of them, getting a real taste of the smaller town Kentucky life, but now that they were actually in the sparsely unpopulated town of Westport, Kentucky, population 261, Kaylie and Mags were feeling a bit out of place. Both the girls wore black spaghetti strap tanks with khaki shorts and flip flops. Mitch and Danny, two college-bound athletes, wore whatever they could find that didn't smell too skunky, which happened to be beer shirts and swim trunks. None of them was dressed for fancy line dancing as they pulled up to the bar booming classic country, gravel crunching under their tires. The bar was actually called *The Bar,* a bar within town limits. The next bar over was only a few miles away, but they didn't care which bar they went to as long as it had alcohol and music. The fly paper hanging like party streamers from the front windows didn't look very festive, but at least there would be beer. Kaylie and Mags tried not to be alarmed as the porch stairs creaked, worrying the rotten wood wouldn't hold them. An old gray-muzzled hound dog attached to a rusty chain lay next to a giant bowl of water. He thumped his tail twice and Mags bent to scratch him behind the ears.

"Good dog."

"Ew, Mags. That dog could have fleas. Don't touch him." Kaylie tugged Mags away from the rheumy-eyed beast, who yawned and exposed one remaining canine. "Somebody should do that dog a favor and just put him down."

"Kaylie!"

"Well, he's only got one tooth. Look at him! How does he even eat?"

"Girls," the boys held the torn screen door open for them, which let in more bugs than kept them out. Standing in the dark doorway, their skin glowed green from the beer signs adorning the walls.

Kaylie and Mags jumped as the door hit them on their butts. So much for chivalry. The boys were already hustling to the bar with their wallets open.

"Idiots." Kaylie hissed. "You never show your wallet to the locals. We're bound to get robbed if they know how much we're carrying." She was a naïve college girl who didn't know anything about Louisville and its residents, good honest folk who went to church on Sundays and everyone knew their neighbor's names.

Kaylie nodded at the few regulars sitting at the far end of the bar, her fingernails digging into Mags' arm. "You're hurting me." Mags pried Kaylie's manicured fingers from her forearm. "Loosen up. At least we're out drinking." Mags smiled at the bartender, an older woman wearing so much silver jewelry she could hardly stand straight. The woman smiled back, which gave her the resemblance of a surprised and aging Kewpie doll. Her eyelashes were furry spider legs and the coral color of her lipstick had bled into the deep smoking lines around her mouth, but her long blonde ponytail was bright and bubbly, bopping to a Dolly Parton song.

They all slid onto sticky bar stools, ripped and showing some stuffing. Beside Mags, a half-eaten melted cheddar cheese sandwich rested on a plate, the grease from the cheese oozing into a fatty puddle. A fly sat cleaning its front legs on the top piece of bread. "Don't order food from the kitchen. There are flies on it," Mags whispered to Kaylie.

Kaylie, titled her head in Mags' direction. "I'm sorry, what were you saying, Mags? Mitchell was talking about going for a swim to cool down later." She winked at Mitch.

"Never mind. I'll have a Coke," Mags said to the bartender.

"What kind of Coke you want, baby?" Her dull blue eyes stared at something crusty she was picking off the bar in front of them with a ruby red fingernail. She met Mags' eyes. "Oh, don' mind that, sugar. It's nothin', just a little salsa Ed dropped from his snack earlier. Won't hurtcha none. I'll get it cleaned up right away. Now 'bout that Coke?" She stood with her hands on her skinny jeans, which were busting at the seams, her nipples poked through the thin fabric of her peach t-shirt she had tied in a knot in back to show off her full figure.

"Yes, I'd like a Coke."

"Well, what kind, darlin'?" The bartender leaned over the dark wood counter. "We've got orange Coke, root beer Coke, Big Red coke, grape Coke, and Coca Cola Coke. Which one do ya want?"

Mags looked confused. "I guess I'll have a Coke Coke. Thank you."

"Name's J.J., honey, an' yer welcome," she said as she slammed the bottle down on the edge of the counter and sent the bottle cap flying. "What can I get yer friend here?" J.J. nodded at Kaylie, who was watching the regulars at the end of the bar as they were watching her. One of them with a graying beard tipped his cowboy hat at her.

"She'll have a beer on the house," Earl piped up.

"Earl, ya flirt with every pretty young thang that walks in that door an' ya know ya always go home to yer wife. Don' mind him, sugar. He don' bite. That's Earl, Harry, an' the one that looks like Willie Nelson we call *One Drink Bill.*" She pointed to the boys. "Don' ask me why. Danged if I know. His name ain't Bill an' he always orders more than one drink. Ha!" Her barky smoker's wheeze sounded as tired as the men at the end of the bar looked. J.J. twisted the cap off a green bottle and slid it across the bar. "Yer boyfriends having the same?" She nodded towards Mitchell and Danny, sliding more green bottles towards them.

Kaylie felt hot breath on the back of her neck. "Ya wanna dance, sweet thang?" It was Earl.

She placed her hand on her neck to protect herself from his hot breath defiling her skin.

"She's with me," Mitch said.

Danny and Mags kept their heads down, but Mags reached out to take Kaylie's hand in hers. Kaylie was shaking.

"Sorry, didn't know," Earl put his hands up and backed away. "She's a cute one." He winked at her and returned to his seat at the other end of the bar.

The door to the kitchen flooded the dark bar with white light. "Mee-Maw." A boy wearing jeans, a white shirt, and a dirty white apron, stepped behind the bar. "I'm hungry." He hung on J.J.'s arm like a little boy.

"This is More Sweet. We call 'im that because he's more sweet than all t'other boys his age. His mama was killed in the car accident that made him differnt." J.J. tapped the side of her head with a fingernail. "He's my sweet boy, as sweet as can be. He won't hurt ya none." She grabbed both his cheeks and kissed him on the lips. "Whatcha hungry for,boy? Mee-Maw will make it for ya in a jiffy." More Sweet swayed as he thought. "Y'all can just call 'im Sweets. We do," she nodded towards the four of them.

"Peanut butter sammich." He went around the bar and sat next to Mags. "Hi. Yer pretty."

"Thank you, Sweets." Mags smiled at him, sliding a little closer on her stool to Kaylie.

"Mee-Maw says I'm Melungeon."

"Oh?" Mags nodded as she drank her bottled Coke.

The revolving kitchen door swung back and forth on its hinges as J.J. set a plate with a sandwich with all the crusts cut off before Sweets.

"Sweets' daddy used to own one of the mountains here 'n Appalachia country 'fore the coal mine bought it from 'im. Sweets' daddy died 'n a mining accident. I'm all he's got now." She patted her heart. "Y'all know 'bout Melungeons? Abraham Lincoln, Tom Hanks, and Elvis Presley were/are all Melungeons. Y'all ain't from 'round here."

"No, ma'am," Danny said.

"Oh, honey, please call me J.J." She grabbed Danny's hand, lingering a little too long. "I promise I don' bite. Unless, yer girlfriend here wants me to." She winked. "Melungeons are the kings an' queens of these mountains an' hollers. Ain't that right, Sweets?"

"Sweets is a king. Yuh," he said, chewing with his mouth open.

"Melungeons had it rough. They came to these here hills an' hollers in the late eighteenth century, a mix of European, red Indians an' black slaves. They've always looked down on us as white trash 'round here, but we worked this land an' lived here longer than most of t'other. Most o' us have French blood. We didn't have that black blood in us. Mama said we didn't. We had blue eyes. That's where the fancy name *Melungeon* comes in. They say we have this bony knob on the back of our head that distinguishes us from other races. My Mee-Maw showed me how to find it when I was a little girl an' I taught Sweets. Sweets, show these people yer bump." Sweets took Mags hand gently. Mags gasped.

"Don' worry. He won' hurt ya."

"It's right here." He guided Mags' hand to a small bump on the back of his head just above the neck.

"Now ya feel yer head an' tell Sweets if ya have a bump," J.J. said, grinning like a clown.

Mags felt the back of her head. "Nope."

"Well, I guess that don' give her the right to spit on us like trash an' order us 'round, does it Sweets? Cuz she ain't mountain royalty like yer an' yer Mee-Maw." J.J. cackled.

"Why don' ya ask Sweets to dance, girl? What's yer name?"

"Mags." Mags looked into Danny's eyes.

"Ask Sweets to dance. He likes to dance with pretty young girls an' we don' get many in here, do we Sweets?" J.J. nodded to her grandson.

"Nup." Sweets smiled at Mags.

Mags took a swallow of her drink and set the bottle down hard on the bar.

"I think we're going to cash out and get going. Got a long drive," Danny said, pulling his wallet out of his pocket.

"Y'all sit back down and finish those drinks," J.J. barked. "Miss Pretty is gonna have a dance with my grandson. Earl," J.J. gestured with a long fingernail, "put on some Elvis. Sweets likes Elvis. Go on, Sweets. Take that girl out for a spin."

J.J. and the three men at the end of the bar guffawed as Sweets stood up and took Mags by the hand and walked her to a tiny square of empty floor between four worn dining tables. He put his hands on her hips and Mags screamed.

Danny lunged. "Don't you hurt her!"

J.J.'s men at the end of the bar were quick to grab him and hold him. "Just let 'im enjoy his dance, son. He ain't gonna hurt her none," Earl said as he spat a plug of tobacco onto the dirty bar floor.

"Mags," Kaylie screamed, standing behind Mitch.

Mitch hopped over the bar in one swift movement and grabbed J.J. by her ponytail, forcing her head to the bar. The click of his .38 was the only sound. "You let my friends go and there won't be any trouble." Mitch made eye contact with Earl and his buddies; the gun trained on them. "I said let her go."

Silence.

Mags felt her pulse racing and the room reeled. Mitch set the gun down out of J.J.'s reach, pulled a lighter out of his pocket, and the snick of the flame made Kaylie cringe. She was standing with her back pressed up against the screen door and her purse strap clutched to her chest. Mitch forced J.J.'s left hand flat on the bar and applied the hot flame to the center of her hand. The stink of burning human flesh filled the air as J.J. wallowed like a hog, struggling to get away, trapped by Mitch, who still had her hair wrapped around his hand like a lasso. He held the gun in his other hand, still pointed it at the men. "Let us go and I'll stop."

The three men released Danny and he ran to Kaylie's side.

"Sweets! SWEETS! Mee-Maw needs ya to let the nice lady go now!" J.J. screamed through gritted teeth as beads of sweat popped out on her brow and her face turned ruddy. Mags ran to Kaylie and Danny. Mitch pointed the gun at the men and backed away from J.J., who was bawling, snot running from her nose.

"You let us leave now and there won't be any more trouble." He kept the gun pointed on the three men as they all backed out of the bar onto the narrow porch.

"Y'all best be leavin' our fine town, cuz if I see y'all again, I'm goin' to slit yer throats an' use yer pretty girls for my bed, ya hear?!" Earl bellowed out the screen door. J.J.'s howls of pain could be heard inside, along with Sweets crying and hollering. The bloodhound didn't even bark as the four kids started up their car and backed up out of the gravel drive, kicking rocks up, as they headed further north.

***

"Why are we stopped here?" Mags held Kaylie in the back seat as she cried on her shoulder, shaking.

"We need to get back before they find us." Mitch turned off the rental and sat beside the calm Ohio River. Moonlight skated across the water. The bank was thick in slippery elm, oak, hemlock, walnut, ash, maple, hickory, and river birch.

"What about the police?" Mags asked as they picked their way down to the bank and found a few fallen logs to sit on.

Mags frowned as Kaylie pulled a pipe out of her pocket and lit up. "Really? We just got molested by the Deliverance Gang and you're going to ride me about a little green?" Kaylie passed Mags the pipe.

"You have a point." Mags shrugged and inhaled.

"No, I meant about the body."

"What body?" The boys laughed.

They all sat around smoking, watching the river, and listening to the night sounds around them for a time, until they felt drowsy. There was no telling how much time had passed, when they heard the distinct crunch of footsteps behind them.

Mags was the first to see him. "It's Sweets," she whispered. "I think he's got a knife."

Sweets stepped out from the cover of the trees to their little gathering on the banks, a shiny meat cleaver in his right hand. "Ya hurt Mee-Maw." He held the meat cleaver in his unsteady hand, advancing on the group.

Mitch laughed. "If you don't get your retarded ass out of here, I'm going to hurt you too, Sweets. Go on. Git!"

Kaylie and Danny laughed along with Mitch, but Sweets stood still as a deer, though the hand with the meat cleaver shook. "N-no. I ain't leavin'."

Mags stood up and approached Sweets with her head lowered and her hands at her sides. "Hey, Sweets. Remember me? I'm Mags." She put her hands out to show she didn't have a weapon.

Before Mags reached Sweets, Mitch and Danny had tackled Sweets to the ground and the meat cleaver went flying. "Get the knife," Mitch shouted. Danny scrambled around, feeling for it in the shadows on the bank. He came back with it in his left hand. "Give it to me."

"Mitch, what are you doing?" Danny looked at his best friend.

"Give me the knife, Danny. Come on," Mitch gestured for the knife.

"No."

"Come on, Danny, it's me, your best friend. Give me the knife."

Danny handed the cleaver over to Mitch, who held Sweets pinned by one scrawny wrist. "Hold him down."

"Mitch—"

"I said hold him down, Danny. Now you're going to hold him down and we're going to teach Sweets a little lesson about what happens to people when they come after us with a knife."

Mags gagged. "Danny, no! Don't do it!"

"Kaylie, why don't you take Mags to the car, okay?" Mitch glowered at Mags.

"Okay. I'll—"

"No. I'm not going to the car. I'm staying right here. Kaylie," Mags pleaded with her girlfriend, "this is ridiculous. Tell Mitch to stop."

Silence. Kaylie held onto Mags' wrist as tears fell from her eyes. Danny was straddling Sweets.

"No, no, no, no, NO!" Sweets was struggling to break free.

"This is what happens to retards like you, big fella. Now this'll only hurt for a second." Mitch raised the cleaver above his head. Danny looked away. The girls and Sweets screamed as the cleaver came down on Sweets' right hand, severing two fingers and partly severing his thumb, which now hung by a strand of skin. The red blood was shiny in the moonlight.

Sweets, fueled by pain and the desperate will to live, bucked Danny off him and managed to punch Mitch in the jaw with his uninjured fist, which sent Mitch and the cleaver flying. Sweets pounced on the cleaver and raised it high in front of him with his good hand. He stood over Danny, who was just getting up.

"Danny, run," Mitch yelled, as he lunged for Sweets and took him down, grabbing his legs in a bear hug. He punched Sweets in the nose and Sweets bellowed.

Mitch felt around for something to use as a weapon and grabbed hold of a rock, which he slammed repeatedly into Sweets' wrist, forcing him to let go of the cleaver. Sweets then bit him, which enraged Mitch even more. In the moonlight, all Mags could see were Mitch's large black pupils, and wet red blood all over him and Sweets. Sweets was moaning and covering his head to protect himself. Mitch took the rock in one meaty hand and yanked back Sweets' arm, slamming the rock repeatedly into Sweets' face. The first few hits produced some popping and cracking and Sweets gurgling as he cried. Then silence. Mitch swung the rock down over and over again. All his friends heard was a mushy thunk. Chunks of brain matter and splotches of blood covered Mitch's face and chest and arms. He couldn't stop hitting Sweets. Tiny pieces of flesh and white shards of bone rained down on both of them.

By the time Danny wrestled his friend to the ground in a bear hug, Sweets' face was a pile of raw dog meat, a red pulpy crater glistening in the moonlight. He wasn't even recognizable.

"Oh my God," Mag screamed over and over. "You killed him! We killed him! Kaylie, we killed him!"

Kaylie held her sobbing, out of control girlfriend, tears running down her face too as her shoulders shook. The two of them clung to each other for shelter to avoid looking at the grotesquerie sprawled on the bank before them.

"We have to cover him. We have to bury him. Okay? We have to bury him. We have to cover him up," Danny kept repeating in a quiet voice. "Mitch." He slapped his friend hard in the face. "Mitch, we have to bury him."

"Yeah. Okay." Mitch took the bottom of his shirt and used it to wipe the blood and brains from his face. "We have to bury him. Okay," he mumbled.

For the next half an hour, Mitch and Danny worked on scraping out an indentation deep enough to lay Sweets in, but the soil by the riverbank was hard and held a lot of clay. They gave up chopping chunks of clay and dirt and rocks with the long, thick branches they used as shovels and finally rolled Sweets into a shallow grave. It was so shallow, half of him still rose above the ground. By now, the two girls had quieted themselves and were huddling together on a log, sniffling and shivering in shock.

"You two," Danny called to their girlfriends. "Come help us cover him with some leaves and branches. We have to hide the body."

"What? Why?" Mags stood up, clutching Kaylie's hand.

"Because we have to hope nobody is going to come looking for him here until sometime after we're in school."

"The local wildlife and bugs will have taken care of him by then and scattered most of him about," Mitch said. "If we're lucky, we haven't left any DNA at the crime scene, but if we did, if we *did*," he emphasized, "we're all in agreement it was in self-defense, right?" Mitch looked into the eyes of each of his childhood friends. "Cuz hopefully, by the time they find this body, we'll have just finished up our first semester of college. And there won't be much left for the police to go on."

"Shouldn't we call the police? What if we told them it was an accident?" Mags asked.

"We are not calling the police, Mags. Come on, let's help the boys." Kaylie grabbed her best friend's hand and they all started pulling pieces of brush and large sticks and scraping up armfuls of moist, decaying leaves covered in beetles and other insects that would hopefully help decompose Sweets, along with the heat of summer. They worked in silence for a long time before they got in the car for the ride back to Louisville.

That fall none of them talked about what happened on their vacation in Louisville, Kentucky. Mitch was the first to die. He mistakenly saw

Sweets and chopped his hands off. Danny got tackled on the football field and broke his back. Before his eyes closed, he got a glimpse of Sweets looking down at him in his football helmet. *But no… It couldn't be.* Mags signed up for the college dance marathon. She made it ten hours in before slipping in someone's spilled water and hitting her head on the stage. She died instantly, but before she did, she saw Sweets smiling down at her. And Kaylie, poor Kaylie, one day she went blind when she was crossing the street and she stepped in front of a car driven by Sweets. He pulled over, smiled, and vanished into the breeze. His job was done.

MURDER HORNET MAN SAVES MILWAUKEE (SORT OF)

For K.W.

I, Keith Justice Hayward, have a gun to my head. This isn't how I planned my evening. Nope. If I die from this shitty stunt, I'm not winning the bet against my best friend, Kurt. As a shitty bonus, I might kick the bucket wearing this stupid fucking costume. Oh, wait! Whose idea was this bet? Kurt's! That motherfucker. Man, if I live through this shit show, I'm going to track Kurt down and just before I smack the crap out of him, give him a colossal piece of my motherfucking mind as to why. Fuck this vigilante hero bullshit and fuck Kurt. Right now, I need to handle the situation, which is kind of hard to do with my face planted against the back of a rusted out 1990 silver Chevy Tahoe with a Darwin fish slapped on the bumper. Props to the Darwin fish. It's having a better night than I am.

Ouch. My temple is aching. Goddamn it. I try to turn my head to see this asswipe, which is an impossible feat in my yellow ski goggles and balaclava.

"Stay down," my attacker orders me, shoving the barrel of the 9mm Ruger harder into my temple. I need no further persuasion.

"Hey, can we talk about this? I take the early train to Madison for work and your gun is seriously impeding my bedtime routine. Also, I'm getting a major tension headache."

"'Scuse me?" The asshole tightens his King Kong grip on the collar of my shirt and doesn't ease up with the Ruger.

"Can we talk about this like two reasonable adults without the gun? And could you please lay off my collar? Dude, you're stretching out my shirt and I just bought it."

Thug dude chuckles at my audacity. "You think you're in a place to be negotiatin'? You're one whacked out cat. I'll give ya that." He flips me around so my back is up against the Chevy's trunk. Right now, I could be home working on my gaming setup. I keep getting bottlenecked with my

Net Dynamo T2 CPU. If I replace the motherboard with a new Hitashi 5.0, I can overclock it. The parts from Amazon are sitting on my kitchen table and it's going to feel like Christmas opening the boxes, if I get out of this clusterfuck alive. I'll be able to play Minesweeper at 144hz on my 6,800p monitors finally. But no, it appears I'm going to spend my last minutes on earth with this motherfucking asshole and his gun.

"Okay. Talk and make it a good story, or I'll shoot ya. An' keep your hands where I can see 'em," my assailant orders, waving his gun in my face. This guy has serious dick issues.

I hope someone will see us and call 911, but my fucking luck sucks worse than the last Godzilla movie. It's two in the morning and all the kitchens adjacent to the alley are closed. Unless someone is late taking out the trash, I'm dying in the middle of October in this alley smelling of piss and rotting kung pao chicken, wearing a black balaclava, bright yellow ski goggles, a black and yellow-striped long-sleeve thermal, black camo cargo pants with black leggings underneath, and brand-new combat boots with bright yellow boot socks. Oh, and four anime collector's ninja throwing stars in a pouch on my belt, which earlier in the evening were badass, but are fucking useless to me now.

"I'll make a deal with you, even though you're obviously the dude in control because *you* don't have the gun pointed in *your* face." I sniff, realizing my new rugged man deodorant has failed me, which adds to my level of my irritation because I have a very keen sense of smell and I paid eight bucks for this shitty organic deodorant without aluminum in it and it can't even make my pits smell good while I die a very cold and violent death.

"Talk." My new friend gestures at me with the gun, appearing bored. Okay, he's a tough sell. I get it. I startle as a rat the size of a chihuahua scurries past us.

"I made a bet with my buddy, Kurt. The loser has to buy the winner the copy of *Superheroes Secret Wars #1* with completely white pages, graded at a 9.8. It's a collector's wet dream and very rare." My voice trails off. It's chilly out, not cold enough to need a jacket, but almost cold enough, and my cat, Zelda, is waiting to be fed at home. "Anyway, the bet is we patrol the back alleys of Riverwest dressed as an original vigilante superhero character, and if we manage to stop a crime in progress and document it, the loser has to buy that comic for the winner. It's just sitting behind the front counter at Collector's Edge. I can hear it calling to me, 'Keith, Keith Justice Hayward, take me home.' So, if you would kindly let me go and maybe take a cell phone pic with me, I can just get out of your hair and be on my way." I glance at my assailant's head. "Okay, I see you don't have any hair." He growls at me. Damn me for having a motor mouth not connected to my brain. "It's cool. It's a good fucking look, man. I bet it works great with the ladies. You must be killing it." My dumbass tongue just keeps tripping over itself as I watch him pick his bottom teeth with one of those green plastic toothpicks, unimpressed and now scowling.

"Why are you dressed like this, man?" He waves his gun at me again, which is causing my blood pressure to rise. I'm glad the lighting in this alley is a dim sulfur yellow, because I might start hyperventilating soon and I find darker rooms soothing in a state of panic.

I stop slouching against the rusted-out Chevy Tahoe and draw myself up to my full height of 5'10." "I'm Murder Hornet Man."

He busts out laughing so hard, his toothpick goes flying out of his mouth, but he still manages to keep that Ruger trained on me. He is one coordinated cocksucker. "Murder fucking who?"

"Murder Hornet Man, sir," I add, thinking respect might help my cause.

"What's up with them goggles?" He grins, flashing a gold tooth. He stinks of tobacco and cheap cologne, the kind of cologne you buy a few squirts of for a quarter at the gas station.

"I'm incognito. A vigilante character like Batman or V. You dig? The balaclava hides my face and the ski goggles are big bug eyes. You know… like a murder hornet."

"Man, I think those things are fake as fuck. Some sort o' gov'ment conspiracy drone. You ever see one?"

"Well, no, but—"

"I ever see one, imma shoot it. *Bam!* Their gov'ment drone won't work so good then, if it ain't flyin'. Ha-HAH!" His laugh ends on an unsettling high note.

At this point, if I wasn't black, I would turn paler than the Easter Bunny and shit rabbit pellets because I'm so scared of what this crazy motherfucker might do, but I don't, *obviously*. I'm too cool for that. Would Murder Hornet Man fold in the face of danger? Fuck, no. This is the way my demented brain works hopped up on adrenaline.

"Fucking Murder Hornet Man. Ha-HAH." He ends his laugh on a high note again, which makes me think he might really be one of those unpredictable crazy ass buggers.

"Sir, ummm. We seem to be at a crossroads where I could go my way and you could go your way." I cross my arms in an "x." "Never the twain shall meet…" *God, I hope I get out of this alive and never meet this guy again.*

"You talkin' Shakespeare on me, Murder Hornet Man?"

"Oh shit, I think that's Mothman," I whisper out the side of my mouth to my attacker.

"He a friend of yours?" The carjacker gestures with his gun. "Man, what the fuck is up with all you bug nerds and your names? Murder Hornet Man, motherfucking Moth—"

My assailant's head is ripped from his body before he can finish his sentence. A blood geyser shoots from his neck as his heart pumps out the last of his life force and his body falls to the ground. I swear, I see the guy's eyes roll from Mothman to me. You know, they've done studies proving the brain lives on after the heart stops. It's possible, truly possible, I am seeing this dude's eyes move.

Then I remember I'm standing in front of motherfucking Mothman! How cool is this? Kurt will never believe me.

"Dude, Mothman, you saved my ass! Thank you so much." I bow samurai style because he's motherfucking Mothman and I don't know what else to do now. I'm hoping he's not thinking of yanking off my head next.

Mothman's eyes glow red in the dim light. The alley is splattered in blood and stinks of iron. The creature's hand is big enough to grab the guy's decapitated head like a basketball. Silent, Mothman holds out the guy's head to me. The blood is no longer pumping from the stump of the dude's neck. I can see it's not a clean rip; part of a jagged clavicle pokes through a piece of pink neck muscle on one side and the skin from the larynx is missing, revealing some nasty-looking thyroid cartilage. *Ew!*

"Hey, do you think I could get a pic of you standing next to me, holding up this guy's head? My friends are never going to believe me, if I don't have a pic to prove it. By the way, I'm a huge fan of yours. Where did you fly in from? Chicago?"

Mothman drops the head on the pavement and it *thunks!* like a bad cinematic sound effect. He flaps his wings and shoots straight up and away. Damn it! My hopes for social media fame and a book deal with a tour die with Mothman's departure, but I can still win the bet against Kurt. Walking through puddles of blood is a lot gorier than it looks in the movies and it's very hard not to leave behind footprints, but I'm determined to get this guy's head and the Ruger. Yeck! I realize it's a bit sad, the lengths I'm willing to go to for a comic book, but then, it's not just any comic. It's a copy of *Superheroes Secret Wars #1* graded at a 9.8, with completely white pages!

I kneel beside the guy's corpse and take the Ruger from his right hand, surprised to find his body still warm. I lose my dinner all over the dude's chest and then I pick up his bloody, decapitated head and carry it under my right pit like a basketball. I plunk it down on the hood of the silver Chevy Tahoe facing away from the windshield, the corpse's glazed eyes staring at me. It looks a bit ooky for a photo, so I take off my yellow ski goggles and stick them on the dude. Much better. For a bit of levity, I take a sharpie from my pocket and draw a mustache and a goatee on his face. I take a moment to compose myself and then I grab the Ruger from the hood of the car and my cell phone from my back pocket and start mean mugging next to the severed head. I snap several pics from different angles with my iPhone, until I'm satisfied with the lighting. Kurt is gonna buy me that damn comic book after he sees this shit. And I'll have a newspaper article to back me up, because some poor soul is gonna find this asshole in the morning when they come to work. I bet he'll smell ripe by then.

I take my shoes off and skate around in the blood puddles to disguise my boot prints, and I check to make sure I haven't dropped my wallet with my ID anywhere. That's always how they get you on *Dateline*. Someone always drops their motherfucking ID and then they're in front of Chris Hanson, crying about how they didn't mean to do it and it was a mistake. A severed head would be hard to explain as a mistake, as would the photos, which I won't be posting anywhere and will be erasing from the cloud after I shove them in Kurt's disbelieving face. I count how many security cameras are in the alley and then I toss my socks into the last dumpster and carry my boots underneath my arm, exiting the alley. My DNA isn't in the system, I'm confident. I pat my back pocket. My cell phone is safe. A black man wandering around barefoot after two o'clock in the morning will look suspicious on camera, though. Speaking of cameras, I'm counting the traffic cameras as I hoof it barefoot back to my pad. I'll be deleting all footage from those cameras and the security cameras in the alley. It's going to be a long morning, hacking into the county system and all those businesses' private camera systems, but I'm a man with a mission.

As I enter my pad, Zelda greets me at the door looking for food. I reach to scratch her behind the ears. My phone rings. I see it's Kurt calling. "Hey, man. How'd your night go?"

"Not too great. Nothing interesting happened. You?"

"Have I got a story to tell you. I'll see you at Murray's tomorrow night."

"Really? You actually stopped a crime?" Poor Kurt sounds butthurt, because he knows he's just lost an expensive bet.

"I did, man. And I've got the pics to prove it and the newspaper should back me up. To the winner go the spoils, Kurt." I grin as I check my face for blood in the bathroom mirror, say goodbye, and hop in the shower.

I wonder if Mothman is on Instagram yet. I should check that out.

DOWN TO THE WATER'S EDGE

Plainfield, Wisconsin is home to 899 poor souls lost in the middle of marsh and farming country. It's also home to the infamous body snatcher and murderer Ed Gein, though if you travel to Plainfield Cemetery, you'll be hard pressed to find his tombstone. The locals gave up replacing that bit of gruesome history years ago and poor Ed lies for all eternity in an unmarked grave, if he's even in that grave.

The wind tousled my long black tresses into fashionable mermaid knots as I tapped the side of my red Toyota Tacoma to the beat of The Cure. Up around the bend, the lake winked into view. I slowed down. I stepped out of my dusty truck and adjusted the wide brim of my black sun hat looking rather striking in my loose black dress, though not a soul was there to witness my entrance into Podunk Ville. The silver ripples on Long Lake, and the humble white Cape Cod with a broad limestone stairway leading to the shore, were reminiscent of my favorite Milwaukee beach. This was not the big city, though. I dropped my luggage on the ground and stretched, inhaling, raising my fingertips to the dusky sky. A raft of ducks took off from the reeds in a flutter of feathers and quacking. The imposing pines surrounded the tiny white house, holding the two-story Cape Cod prisoner beneath their stalwart branches. I lowered my large black sunglasses as I approached the front porch, crunching pine needles beneath my boots and worried the key on the shoestring around my neck as I shouldered my luggage and laptop and clomped up the uneven wooden steps. They were in need of painting like everything else around here. Cleaning a dirty window with the sleeve of my dress, I peeked inside.

Downstairs was a plain wood table with four chairs off to the left, a behemoth of a plaid sofa in front of the fireplace in the center of the room, and a rocking chair next to one of the windows overlooking Long Lake. I'd only found out about my great aunt's death last week, but here I was ready to scare up some ghosts. It was nearing Samhain. Maybe, I could invite Dina and Raini up next weekend and we could have a rousing séance in the October cold.

Thankfully, the estate appraiser mentioned a half-cord of firewood stored on the west side of the house. I prayed to the Goddess of Rodents that all the mice had left the premises, merry and *never* to meet here again. I entered the shadowy house, dropped my stuff beside the couch, and went exploring for a light switch. Lucky me, I hit my shin on a table as I passed the couch.

"Goddess damn it!" The lamp fell off the table and the shattering of glass almost made me cry. I hoped it wasn't a pretty lamp.

In the waning rectangle of light from the open front door, I managed to find the light switch, reveling in the glory of industrial light for about two seconds before I heard a tiny fizzle, then a pop, then smelled burnt wiring. I needed to get an electrician out here on Monday. Unfortunately, it was only Friday night. Now I was hoping Great Aunt Tillie, called Tillie by everyone that knew her, was a practical lady and kept candles and matches someplace downstairs.

The logical place to look was the fireplace mantel, which is where I found a useful collection of vintage bed chamber candlestick holders, an unused box of plain tapers, a box of strike anywhere matches, and a kerosene lantern, half-filled. Thank the Goddess! Now I could get a good fire going, which I assumed would be the only heat in the little Cape Cod. I struck a match and lit the kerosene lamp to investigate upstairs.

The stairs creaked as old stairs do, but I didn't mind. The house was talking to me. I was becoming acquainted with my new friend and imagined many hours spent writing and hiking and taking photographs. After the past year, recovering from a breakup with my narcissistic girlfriend, I relished isolation and adventure. I'd never been a house owner, always a renter with a roommate or lover, never staying in one place too long. At the top of the landing, I paused to look out the window, admiring the original glass with the warps and bubbles. Well, I had a few of those too, so we'd get along fine, this old house and me. It spoke to my soul. I lifted the kerosene lantern to the darkened window. The thick pine trees obscured my view. I'd go exploring tomorrow.

Great Aunt Tillie's bedroom was down a short, efficient hallway to the left. The furnishing was simple, a double bed covered in a homemade quilt, a missionary style wardrobe, and a cedar chest at the foot of the bed that held extra blankets and linens. The air was musty. I would open windows tomorrow to remedy this, but I could tolerate it for one night. Hand-tied rag rugs lay on the white painted wood floor, and I was grateful for them as I slipped out of my shoes and settled on the bed, which blessedly did not creak like so many things in Great Aunt Tillie's home.

I turned off the kerosene lamp, too tired to care about undressing or starting a fire in the fireplace and slipped under the quilt. The linens smelled faintly of rosewater. I drifted off to sleep listening to the house settling around me. The last sound I heard before closing my eyes was a lone owl in the pines.

***

I wore a plain white nightgown with a boxy neckline. My brow was feverish. My sweat smelled sour. A brown bottle of morphine sat on the nightstand. The bedroom walls were a hideous shade of green, somewhere between calf-shit green and vomit chartreuse. My throat felt swollen shut. Large, painful canker sores covered my tongue and the roof of my mouth. I tasted salt and coughed blood into a white handkerchief. A pretty rosy-cheeked girl in a white button-down blouse and pants sat reading *The Angel of Ghosts* by Edgar Wallace beside my bed. Fanny Brice crooned "My Man" over the tombstone-style crystal radio. Beads of moisture collected on the outside of a full pitcher of water, so cold, but I couldn't drink anything. My clammy pillow stuck to my unruly chin-length bob. I held my hand to my burning, swollen jaw and opened my mouth to speak, but instead began another coughing fit. This time I ended up with a bloody molar in my hand.

***

I awoke with a beast of a headache, grinding my teeth, my fists clenched, and my brow moist, though the air in the room was rather chilly. The left side of my face felt hot and swollen, like I had an impacted tooth. I lit the kerosene lamp and saw a spot of blood on the embroidered pillowcase. I padded in my stockinged feet to the wardrobe where a full-length mirror hung inside and patted my face. The excruciating pain disappeared immediately, which alarmed me. My cheeks were pale, not swollen and flushed. I still had all my teeth. *Odd.*

I crawled back under the quilt, leaving the kerosene lamp burning to chase away my nightmare. There was no blood on my pillowcase either. I checked. My eyelids grew heavy again.

I don't know how long I was asleep the second time when I awoke to the ticking of an old-fashioned alarm clock. I sat up in bed and listened for the direction it was coming from, which was by the window overlooking Long Lake. Strange, because there was no clock over there, but I got out of bed to investigate. A very faint glow emanated through the cracks in the floorboards. Thumping my hand along the boards, I discovered one board was looser than the others and managed to pry it up. I shone the kerosene lamp inside the secret compartment and discovered an alarm clock radiating a green glow from the face. I lifted it out. It was quite heavy and vintage. I wondered why it was tucked away beneath the floorboards and that's when I caught a flash of white out of the corner of my eye. I pulled a hefty packet of letters addressed to Tillie from Frankie. The thick bundle was dog-eared and tied with a wide grosgrain ribbon of dusty peach. I set the alarm clock and the bundle of letters on the bedside table and crawled back into bed. The air was so chilly I could see my breath, and I remembered I hadn't started the fireplace. Damn. The ticking of the alarm clock punctuated the silence and I tossed and turned the rest of the night.

***

It had stopped. I yawned and reached to wind the clock. I woke up with the weak morning light of autumn streaming through the window and made a mental note to add blackout curtains to my list of shopping items. The clock appeared to have sprung a spring in the middle of the night, which was a shame, since it was so beautiful. I discovered an engraving on the back. *Counting the minutes.*

I went downstairs and brought my bags up, rummaged around for my toiletries, and then remembered there was no electricity, which probably meant no water, because she had a well. *Damn!* I opted for my favorite black leggings and oversize chunky knit sweater, chewing a bit of toothpaste and spitting it into a tissue. *Gross.* Not wanting to bother with my hair, I found a pair of chopsticks and fashioned a loose and messy bun. By then my stomach was grumbling, so I Googled mom and pop diners and found Misty's Menu, which looked, from the online reviews, like they had the perfect comfort food and cheap diner coffee I adored. Grabbing the bundle of letters, I decided to walk to breakfast, since it was a nice sunny morning.

***

Misty's Menu was a little hole in the wall diner painted forest green with lots of dead animal heads staring at me while I read the letters. After five cups of coffee, I was about to float away. On the way to the john, I bumped into my waitress.

"Excuse me, miss." She performed an expert waitress weave around me in the narrow hallway, snapping her gum.

I looked at her nametag on her drab brown uniform. "Cindy, is there a historical society for the town nearby? I just inherited my Great Aunt Tillie's place and I'd like to find out more about the area."

"Oh, the Marsh place. Everyone loved Tillie Marsh. She was a sweetheart. Of course, we have a historical society, though if you ask me, they're pretty stuffy—all members of the D.A.R." I looked bewildered. "Daughters of the American Revolution. You're not from around here; I can tell. It's okay." She continued gabbing in the way small towners do, but eventually she got to the directions. "Turn right out of the parking lot and then left at the barn with the smiley face. It'll be on the left side of the road next to the candy store with the giant bear out front. Ask for Pearl or May. They're the town keepers of everything. You have a blessed day now."

Right. Left at the barn. Next to the big bear. I smiled and thanked her. After using the john, which boasted it was the world's largest taxidermy bathroom in *The Guinness Book of World Records*, I headed toward my destination. I found the bear, but didn't win a prize for Miss Congeniality as I yelled and flapped my arms at a rafter of turkeys moseying down the middle of the road like it was a lazy Sunday afternoon.

I walked into the storefront of the tiny strip mall. It smelled of coffee and sugar cookies. Pictures of the town from a hundred years back plastered every inch of wall not dedicated to the dark and solemn bookcases moping in their musty paper scent. I didn't blame them. The stagnant store could use some pops of color, a few potted plants, and a good smudging. The floorboards sighed as I rang the shiny bell at the front desk.

Two thick women popped their heads from the backroom. One piebald lady wore a patchworked prairie dress and the other, younger one wore sensible slacks and a navy floral print blouse. "Can we help you?" they asked in unison.

Okay, that's not creepy. I shifted my messenger bag on my shoulder. "I was looking for some information on the old Tillie Marsh place."

"Ah." The lady in the prairie dress adjusted her large square glasses. "You must be Tillie Marsh's great niece."

"Word travels fast in a small town," the other woman explained at my surprised smile.

"Yes, I'm Shabbi. I recently inherited the place, and I found these letters under a floorboard in the bedroom." I pulled the bundle out of my bag, placing them on the counter. Oddly, I felt them shift in my hands. I slid them across the counter.

"Ah," the one in the glasses nodded. "The Frankie letters. That's a sad story." She glanced at her friend Pearl. "I'll put on some tea. Would you like some?"

"None for me, thank you. I just came from the diner."

"Thank you, May. Have a seat, Shabbi." Pearl gestured to a sitting area with three overstuffed green chairs. She took a cracked leather photo album from a bookcase, turning the pages to pause on a picture of a pretty young brunette with a wavy flapper hairstyle hidden by a hat, and a print dress. A tall skinny blonde woman with a short pageboy smiled next to her, her eyes burning with conviction. She wore knickers, well-worn leather boots, and a button down shirt, unusual for the time.

Pearl set her own teacup down when she came back with a tray of black English tea and peach tea. She poured a cup for May.

"Thank you, May."

"Frankie," Pearl pointed to the tomboy, "was best friends with Tillie. Tillie's parents owned a farm not far from the Marsh place and the girls were thick as thieves. One day, Tillie's brother caught the two of them kissing and holding hands in the hayloft. As you can imagine, being like that back then was not accepted. Tillie was engaged to Chester, one of the farmhands, but her heart had always belonged to Frankie from the time they both could walk. Tillie and Frankie had planned on running away together before Tillie's wedding in May and riding the rails until they found a place that felt like home." Pearl paused to sip her tea. The peach steam wafting through the air reminded me of the peach grosgrain ribbon binding the letters. I could feel the ghost of a girl's kiss on my lips.

May continued the story. "Chester and the boys, including Tillie's brother, decided to teach the two girls a lesson. Tillie's brother held her down while Chester had his way with his future bride. Frankie was forced to watch, held in check by two of the other farmhands. She cursed and fought and screamed as Tillie's shrieks rose to the rafters, but Frankie wasn't able to break free. Folks said when Chester was done with Tillie, he spat in her face and told her to put her dress on and go home. He said that she was his and no bull dyke would ever touch her again."

"*You'd best remember that, Tillie,* folks quoted Chester screaming at her backside as she stumbled home shoeless, blinded by tears, her hair in knots and snot running down her face."

"Then the boys turned on Frankie," May said quietly, not able to meet my gaze, as a single tear burned in the corner of my left eye. "They forced Frankie to perform fellatio on all of them while they watched and jeered, said once she learned what a dick tasted like she'd never want a woman's"—May blushed and paused—"pussy. Then they beat her up and ran her out of town. Destitute and with no relatives willing to take her in, Frankie rode the rails for a while, until she healed. Then she passed herself off as a young man and went off to fight in World War I in Europe. She wrote to Tillie every day she was overseas, not knowing Tillie was pregnant with Chester's baby. Chester refused to marry Tillie because she wasn't a virgin, no matter that it was he who got her pregnant. Tillie's father, Billie, got her a job as one of them radium girls painting clock and watch dials that glowed in the dark, but he said after the baby was born, he wanted nothing to do with her or it and she would have to find another place to live. Tillie's mother was heartbroken. She died shortly after Frankie was run out of town, and some say it was Tillie's dalliance that killed her.

"Heartsick too and pregnant, with no prospects of marriage or any place to go, Tillie worked at the radium dial factory for the war effort, until she took ill a few months later."

Pearl interrupted, "You see, the radium paint made the girls sick. They were instructed to lick the tips of their paintbrushes to keep a fine point. The paint ingested from the brushes caused horrible growths, ulcers of the mouth, tongue, and throat; the girls' teeth rotted and fell out, their jaw bones ached and weakened, eventually falling apart. They couldn't eat and suffered excruciating pain until death."

"When Tillie realized she was poisoned, she was only a few months pregnant. One night she got up and walked out of the house, down the steps, and into the lake to take her last breath. She's often seen by young women in her white nightgown walking down to the water's edge. The locals call her *The Woman in White.*"

"I found an old alarm clock upstairs," I said.

"Yes," May nodded. "She was saving that clock for her baby's birth. It was all she had to give him or her. That morning Tillie's brother and father found her floating, arms outstretched, staring skyward, her white nightgown spread like a sail around her, her lips blue, and a smile on her face. Her father, Billie, kept that clock on the mantel from then on. He was so ashamed he hadn't saved his baby girl. He never spoke her name again, until the day he died twenty years to the day Tillie took own her life.

Some say the last word Ole Billie uttered was *Tillie*. And then he smiled and took his last breath. Your family bought the house after his death."

"And what happened to Frankie?" I shifted in my chair.

"No one knows," Pearl shook her head. "Some say she took her own life when she learned of Tillie's passing. Some say she rode the rails for a few years until she settled in Kansas after the war, but she never came back home again."

I slipped the letters back into my messenger bag and stood. "Thank you." I didn't know what else to say. Melancholy wrapped itself around me like a sullen cloak.

***

I walked back to the house silent, my hands curled in fists so tight my knuckles hurt. I took the chair from in front of the window and carried it down to the lake, sitting there with the letters in my lap, fingering the wide grosgrain ribbon until dusk painted the sky lavender blue and a lone mourning dove cried out from the pines. Then I took the chair back inside and ate a dinner of cold canned beans by the light of the kerosene lantern and went up the creaky stairs to bed.

Shadows flickered and died, as I extinguished the lantern's flame and slipped beneath Great Aunt Tillie's quilt. I tossed and turned for a while, listening to the house breathing around me, until I finally fell asleep.

Sometime later, I awoke, cold. "Shabbi," a woman sighed. The clock! It was ticking! The hour pointed to three, the numerals glowing phosphorescent in the dark. I shot up out of bed, Was I alone? I took the clock in my hands and felt it stir like the letters. *Strange.* I walked downstairs out the white wooden door in time to the ticking of the clock, barefoot in my Ramones t-shirt, and down the paint-peeling steps to the rough limestone stairs leading down to the water's edge. The stones were ice cold, the clock warm in my hands. I saw Tillie at the water's edge, *The Woman in White,* her pregnant body curved and beautiful, her white nightgown plastered to her fair skin, water streaming from her dark hair. She smiled and beckoned to me, one hand on her belly. "Shabbi," she whispered.

I felt no fear as I approached her, only a mother's love. "Tillie." I was crying. She reached for the clock and cradled it like a newborn in the crook of one arm and with her other hand, her fingertips traced the tear tracks on my cheeks, leaving behind a warm, golden flush that radiated through my body. She turned away from me then, still cradling the clock in one arm, her other arm curled around her belly as she stepped out into the lake, and with one last look back at me, she sank beneath the black water.

A wind stirred in the pines and Tillie's loving voice whispered *thank you* on the evening breeze. The mourning dove cried again, and I shivered as I turned back towards the house and my bed. On Monday I would call for an electrician.

***

On Monday the electrician came. "I'll just take a look in the basement and see what I can find. These old houses usually have wiring needing replacing. That's something you'll have to put on your list of things to do."

The electrician clomped down the stairs. As he did, he thought he saw something glowing phosphorescent in the dark. He walked toward it with his flashlight. It was an old diary, so old the ink had faded to a reddish brown. He opened it out of curiosity and then felt guilty, so he took it back upstairs to Shabbi.

"Miss, I found this diary in the basement on the floor."

"Oh, thank you. This was my Aunt Tillie's house, and I haven't had time to explore everything because the electricity went out." She took the diary from him. The leather was cracked and so old, some flaked away. The cursive inside was so perfect, not messy like hers. She took it to the rocking chair, which seemed a fitting place to read, and as she did, the familiar ticking of the clock started. But how could that be? Her aunt had taken that into the lake with her. Shabbi read:

My darling baby. Long Lake is the perfect place for a daughter to grow up. I know you're a daughter because I can feel you crying in my bones for the shame only a woman can feel for what happened to me that day with Chester and his friends and for my eternal love, Frankie. She will be so happy to meet you, my sweet little pea. If anyone ever finds this book, they will know how much I adore you too. This world is not for us. We're going to go meet Frankie on The Other Side. In my heart of hearts I feel her beckoning to me. Somewhere on the rails I know she passed and I long to feel her touch again. The three of us will have a wonderful life. Whoever is reading this, don't cry for me. My life is about to begin, and I won't be in pain anymore. My daughter Willow, as I've named her, which means grace and elegance, and Frankie and I will be a family, a real family, as God intended us to be.

Love,
Emily (Tillie)

CHASING RABBITS

Gavin took the blind turn on Cody Drive at twenty-five miles per hour, the top down on his convertible, Modest Mouse blaring, the sun warm on his face. It was an early Friday off and he was headed to the lake. He didn't see the rabbit huddled in the middle of the road. It had no time to react as it hunkered down, its wet black eyes shiny with horror.

"Shit!" He attempted to swerve as the rabbit leapt in the direction of his front tires. He felt a hollow thump as the convertible clipped it. He winced and pulled over to the gravel shoulder.

The rabbit lay in the road, a limp bundle. As he approached, he saw it still struggling to breathe, one back leg twitching in the air. He knew nothing could be done for the poor creature, but he couldn't leave it in the middle of the road to be hit again.

The rabbit watched him with liquid black eyes. Up close, Gavin saw a thin line of blood on its muzzle. He knelt. Its fur was ticked a few muddy colors, not just one shade of brown, so it could blend into its natural habitat.

The rabbit accepted her fate, allowing him to cradle her in his hands. He carried it to the thick green grass of the culvert. A car coasted by, the curious driver watching him kneeling in the grass beside a lump of brown fur. Gavin ignored the onlooker, placing his right hand on the rabbit's side. Her teats were swollen. Her body was warm and her fur was the softest thing he'd ever felt. She faded in less than a minute. She had not suffered, but Gavin remained there a few minutes more, his hand on her fur, noting the reflection of the pine trees in her round, black eyes. "I'm sorry," he whispered to the mother. He stood in one single motion and left her there in the ditch, peaceful, like she was sleeping. He drove away, taking the slower way home, no longer feeling like going to the lake. The sound of the tires hitting her body played over and over in his head and he could still feel her beneath his hand as he drove back to his downtown loft.

***

The loft was empty without Allison and his daughter. He had no purpose. His days and nights blurred into one long, exhausting hour. The alimony met his basic needs. He hadn't worked since Tasha was born and Allison went back to graduate school. He spent his days wandering the city streets on foot and his nights riding a martini buzz and popping benzos like candy. He'd crash on the couch and eat a dinner of gin-soaked olives while watching cryptid and paranormal documentaries on YouTube. He'd wake at three a.m. almost every night and stumble to his messy bed, where he wrestled with the sheets and his demons until the sun shone in bars across his face.

"Daddy?" Her voice crackled through the baby monitor he couldn't bear to unplug. It was the last tangible connection to his daughter.

Gavin woke instinctually, stumbling to his daughter's empty nursery at three o'clock in the morning to lift her pillow from the crib. He put it to his face, inhaling her sweet toddler scent, and screamed like a dying animal into her pillow. Where the pillow had been a small pile of rabbit droppings lay. He blinked and leaned into her crib, grabbing one of the droppings, rolling it in his fingers; it felt hard. He dropped it back into the crib. *What sick fuck would leave rabbit droppings in his dead daughter's crib?*

The baby monitor crackled. The sound of a car engine revved. He dropped the pillow on the floor, following the monitor's cord with shaking hands to the wall socket, a safety line to reality. *Still plugged in.* Gavin yanked the monitor from the wall and the plug coiled on the floor like a snake waiting to strike. He collected the sheets from his daughter's crib, shaking the rabbit pellets into the laundry garbage can before putting her sheets on the hot cycle. Someone was playing a cruel joke on him.

Gavin mixed another cold gin martini. It slid down his throat like melted snow and spread warmth through his chest as he felt the terrorized beast in his belly uncurl. He chased the expensive gin with a few benzos and another gulp. It smelled like pine and reminded him of the rabbit. He popped a Vicodin to halt the migraine digging its claws into the base of his skull. Gavin realized he hadn't eaten in over twenty-four hours. *Do not take with alcohol*, the scripts warned. He smirked and dumped the orange bottles into his pajama pockets. Peering over the trash can, he saw the rabbit pellets were gone. His pills rattled like a junkie's teeth in a bottle as he headed to the long galley kitchen.

The cool light of the fridge accentuated the shadows under his eyes. Gavin removed a fresh carton of eggs and grabbed the red frying pan from the overhead rack. He expertly cracked three at once, a neat trick his daughter Tasha clapped for every time. The gin raced up his throat with a viper's bite as he stared down into the sizzling pan. Inside a double bloody yolk, an aborted rabbit fetus curled like a half-formed fleshy pink shrimp with stunted ears and twisted, clawless back feet. Dark maroon shreds of placenta clung to its shiny wet body.

"What the fuck?" Gavin dashed to the sink and puked up the gin and pills. He drank straight from the faucet. The chlorinated water did nothing to rinse the acrid taste out of his mouth. His throat felt raw.

He looked the other way as he scraped the eggs into the sink and ran the disposal, trying not to think of it gobbling the pink mutilated fetus or the nursing mother he'd killed. The thin line of blood on her muzzle glowed in his memory, along with her liquid black eyes reflecting the pines as she took her last breath.

Obviously he was hallucinating. Rabbits didn't pop out of eggs and his daughter had been dead a few months. He knew that. He also knew it was bad to chase his pills with gin, but he couldn't scrub the graphic image of the aborted rabbit fetus in the double yolk, blood red and sunny side up in a quivering egg white. His gag reflex kicked in hard, but nothing was left.

There's no way he'd heard Tasha's voice, and he didn't have a pet rabbit. This was just his sick brain taking him on a crazy carnival spin. Gavin deserved it. He knew he deserved it. He'd been careless and now somewhere a nest of newborn rabbits waited with empty bellies, cold and vulnerable to predators invading the nest. They'd all die. It wasn't her fault. She'd been a good mother. Allison had been a good mother too and a good wife, but he'd fucked it all up. Just like he fucked up the morning Tasha died. If he'd heard her crying on the monitor, her fading wails turning into wheezing pleas while he slept off his gin night out. It didn't matter that it was a freak accident, Tasha's lung collapsing while he slept. His fault his wife knelt howling as clods of dirt pelted Tasha's shiny white coffin. It didn't matter that the turn in the road on the way to the lake was blind and there's no way he could have seen the mother rabbit crossing. It was still his fault because he chose to go to the lake.

He'd been drinking. *Just one more for the road*, he'd told himself. Now she'd come back to haunt him or God was punishing him for his selfishness or the devil was egging him on to his death, no pun intended, or his daughter's spirit was back to avenge her death by driving him batshit crazy, but he didn't believe it was Tasha. Not his sweet baby daughter. *Oh God.* He sat and wept on the couch in front of the television, spilling his martini down his wrist. Not his sweet baby daughter. He remembered the feel of her soft, chubby fingers latching onto his and the way her pigtails shook as she giggled.

He was a coward. A worm. He couldn't even be there to view his daughter's body on the coroner's table, to hold his wife as she sobbed, "No, not my baby! Not my baby!" He heard her from the lobby. No, he deserved to be haunted while his wife slept in the bed where they had created life, when they were still together.

A bunny's scream ripped the night in two. His muscles tensed, his heart a fragile beast ready to shatter in someone's fist. Every part of him turned hot and cold. Was this really happening? Gavin pressed his forehead against the cool steel of the fridge. He flattened his palms against the door. This was real. His heart felt like a balloon torn away by a gust of wind. Bright explosions of light erupted in his periphery vision. Sweat dripped from his hairline, down his cheek, and behind his ear. His chest tightened. He struggled to taste the air and the keening split his head. He put his palms to his face and slapped his cheeks.

Get a hold of yourself, Gavin. It's the meds and the booze yapping. Damn it! He punched the fridge and turned to the sink to splash cold water on his face. A blur of fur scampered around the corner into the living room. He chased the rabbit. Nothing. He searched the room.

Someone let a goddamn rabbit loose in his apartment. He was sure of it. *Fuck.* He needed another pill to level out. *Just one. Okay. Maybe four. It'd been a rough trip.* Couldn't even take a drive to the beach without being reminded of his shitty life. *Fuck.* He'd call his doctor tomorrow. The emergency number if he had to do it. Tell them he'd slipped down the rabbit hole. Chasing the rabbit. White pills. White tails. When had a piece of tail not gotten him in trouble? Was it getting hotter?

Was that—? Was that what he thought it was? No. It couldn't be. Under the pillow, poking out from the corner. Allison's lucky purple rabbit's foot keychain. The rabbit's malformed foot in the yolk. The dirty white rabbit's foot his cat fetched; the gnawed wet fur pulled back from the brass fastener. Feet used for hopping, severed. Bloody skinned rabbits hanging in his grandfather's barn. The overhead light closed in on him like a giant hand strangling his larynx. More flashes of white light. He wheezed. The night his father had his heart attack he heard the coyote's kill. He was chasing the rabbit. They were all chasing rabbits like a pack of hungry dogs. He was just chasing rabbits too.

CEMETERY TACOS ON WEDNESDAY

For Jeffrey Wischer, William DeGrave, and Jerome Starr killed on July14, 1999 in Milwaukee, Wisconsin while building the new Milwaukee Brewers Stadium

My heart felt full to bursting. I felt so much love for humanity or it could have been the lack of oxygen. I imagined it floating high up and away, a red balloon dancing on the end of a taut string. There was no pain, only bliss as I lay beneath the maples and elms in the refreshing shade. Sunlight sifting through their branches warmed my cheeks. I would not cry, even though I felt myself fading from a large gash in my side, one of my spiracles damaged.

I comforted myself amidst the screaming sirens and bleating horns. I was in good company lying amongst the stones of Calvary Cemetery. I thought of all the things humans had that I adored, like cotton candy melting like sweet nectar on the tip of my tongue, the tiny balls of fur curled up at my feet, humming like bees as they gave me kisses with their little pink tongues. And best of all, the kaleidoscope Pan got me for my first earth rotation around the sun, bright carnival colors blooming inside the tube as I watched through the peephole and turned it patiently. I pumped my abdomen, attempting to draw in oxygen faster to no avail. My side was pierced from the accident. It would not be long now. I would follow Pan into the cosmic stardust. My eyelids flickered open as a large shadow loomed over me, his head encompassed by a halo of sunlight, his pink mohawk the color of impatiens in July. It was him, the man who came alone to the cemetery every Wednesday to eat tacos.

***

There's no way to measure how much pain humans experience. I can't bear the teardrops running down their faces or their bellowing like wounded animals. Sometimes I can smell the dead silence clinging to their skin, a cloying saccharine perfume of carnations, lilies, and roses scenting their breath like casket sprays, but I never really look inside them, though they say the eyes are the windows to the soul. I can never lift their lids like tiny wooden shutters when they are resting and see inside them the gaping emptiness where there should be a hole inside another hole where their heart beats because while you think grief leaves an emptiness as vast as an ocean and you cannot swim to the other side, for me the emptiness has weight, so you see, it is not an empty hole. It has mass. It sits heavy as a lodestone upon my chest and anchors my spirit to the ground with an aching tether that cannot and will not ever end. And with each painful breath, I am reminded of the emptiness of that empty hole pressing down on me where my heart used to be. It's not even that mourning is a parasite sucking you dry of all other emotions. You forget how to laugh, to smile. It rips your heart out by the bloody root and leaves you helpless, consumed by a horrible toxin pumped into your veins by miniscule grubs and no matter how many tears you shed, you cannot flush it from your system. You face your reflection every day in the mirror, sunken eyes, your cheeks raw and red from grief. You fall asleep into a yawning black pit of despair and awake the next day with a jolt, realizing you must do it all over again. It leaves a bitter taste in the back of your throat.

I learned this firsthand the night I lost my friend Pan. That night in June wasn't chilly for humans, but for us, it was freezing. We huddled together in front of a drum fire, our wings wrapped close for warmth, antennae drooping. I held in my lap the *Peterson Field Guide to Moths of Northeastern North America*, its binding duct taped, the pages smudged and worn from multiple readings.

"Pan, tell me how many types of moths are in Wisconsin."

Pan sighed. "1,500 types of moths live in Wisconsin, Flora. But what difference does it really make?"

The fire snapped and crackled, sending up tiny orange embers into the dark. Shadows of other people grew large on the warehouse wall as they sat talking around their own fire barrels. We stayed in the back, in the darkest part of the abandoned warehouse with all the rats and dripping water, a place no one wanted to sleep.

"They remind me of home."

"But this isn't our home, Flora. They're not like us."

"You don't find it a bit magical that we both have wings? Just a little? It's possible we could have been one species at one time, Pan."

"No. We aren't like them. We don't kill. We don't steal. And we don't torture innocents for our own pleasure. We're different. From a different place, a different time."

"I think humans are lovely."

"It's dangerous for you to get too close to them. They don't understand what we're trying to accomplish. They think we're monsters when really, we were chosen as guardians of this planet, to protect them, to help them so they can learn and evolve for the war that is coming, the war between Light and Dark Beings. Any time we show ourselves, we end up in the supermarket tabloids and online." He held up his arms, his handsome striated moss green and salmon wings shivering as he gestured. "Mothman sighted in Point Pleasant, West Virginia before the Silver Bridge collapse, killing 46 people in 1967. In 1999 he was sighted in Rockford, Illinois, and he's been repeatedly seen there and in Wisconsin sometimes too. Nobody listens, Flora. What good is it to have premonitions if we can't communicate with them? They just want to shoot us with a dart gun and put us behind bars like the poor beasts in their zoos."

"Well, I believe our similarities are what link us to the Ancestors. We are all one."

"It's late. The sun's up. You should get some sleep." Together, we huddled by the wondrous tangerine glow of the fire as dawn poked her weary head over the horizon in the distance.

***

Flora awoke with a start, dark billows of grey smoke like ghosts' fingers stretching towards the ceiling. Children whimpered and mothers called out in Spanish and English. She turned in a tight circle, searching for Pan. The sooty air stung her nose like a million bee stings and her red eyes watered. Barefoot, she limped across hot, broken glass strewn across the floor, calling out for Pan. She found him collapsed at the back of the warehouse, a giant beam pinning him to the cement.

"Pan." Flora paced in front of him, coughing, holding her hand over her nose and mouth, her beautiful red hair capturing the dance of the fire. "We need to get you help."

He shook his head. He could not speak, but she saw in his face the incredible pain he was suffering. He smiled for her, but it came off as more of a wince. "You need to get out of here, Flora. Get to safety. Go to the cemetery. I'll find you there." His tears washed clean tracks down his sooty cheeks.

Flora knelt and held Pan's hand for a moment in her own, remembering how those strong hands had lifted her into the apple tree as a child and how they taught her to tie her shoelaces. Her shoes! She'd forgotten to put them on before looking for Pan. Her feet bled.

"Tear a piece of my pant leg, Flora, and wrap up your feet. You're hurt."

As he said this a huge *snap!* filled the building; embers flew like strange insects from the ceiling. They lit on his wings and scorched black holes in them. The smell was terrible. Flora almost gagged. "We have to get you out of here, Pan!" She coughed again, hurrying to tie her feet with the cloth as her friend suggested. She knelt beside him and tried to push the beam from his back, but she could not.

"You have to go now, Flora. Go to the cemetery. I'll meet you there."

"Okay." She bowed her head of crimson waves to hide her tears. She would be brave for Pan. She would be brave for herself. As she turned and walked away, her eyes burned amber in the shadows of the flames.

***

Piercing pain nipped like fire ants at her feet with every step Flora took. In all the commotion and the coming sirens, nobody noticed the strange Mothgirl with the red eyes and rag-wrapped feet. She stumbled three city blocks and then, with the last of her strength, pulled herself over the chain link fence like a pole jumper vaulting. She knocked all the air out of her abdomen with a big *woof!* She lay still for a few moments, watching the clouds race across the moon and listening to the sirens and the commotion from the warehouse. Her eyes burned worse than the time she got poison ivy and spent a week with socks on her hands being scolded for scratching. Her lips were split and bleeding. Her tongue was prickly as a thistle, her throat was so dry. She looked around for water and saw one of the old-fashioned pumps maintenance used to draw water for the flowers people planted. The water tasted of iron and pennies, like the ground. It was lukewarm from the pump, having sat in the sun all day. Flora drank and drank until her belly was full, rinsing the soot from her eyes and mouth as best she could. Then she started shivering. Shock was setting in. She had no fire, no blanket, and no shelter. If she didn't find shelter soon, she might not wake up in the morning. What would the humans think then, if they found a giant girl with moth wings dead on the lawn?

She limped through the graveyard to the older section at the back where the honeysuckle smelled the strongest. Here there were many crypts. Pan had explained what the crypts were used for, and while she did not relish spending the night in one, she was sure an old lady's bones wouldn't refuse her shelter. She shook the handles of three, the chains rattling louder than her teeth in her head, before she found one that was open. The door creaked louder than a pair of new sneakers, but inch by inch, with Flora holding her shoulder against the cold stone, she managed to open it enough to allow her entry.

Flora didn't want to go inside. What would she find in there? A mummy? A ghost? A rotting corpse with eyes swollen out of its head like marbles? She shrank back from the entrance, opting to find something to use as a blanket before she went inside. Limping beside the chain link fence under the waxing crescent moon, there was enough light to see by as her moth vision adjusted to the monochromatic blue-black shadows of the cemetery. Ahead, she tore a painter's tarp from behind a crypt. She swaddled herself, finding the pressure of the tarp to be soothing wrapped around her. She limped her way back to the open crypt, her long, delicate fingers trailing the chain link fence. The clean, sharp scent of lavender was too much for her belly to ignore and, kneeling along the fence, she drank her fill before stumbling into the crypt.

The interior of the crypt was dark but for one small arched window on the back wall. There were brass doors for cremains on either side of the crypt, dusty with cobwebs and layers and layers of spiders, but insects didn't bother her. The dead did, though. In the center of the stone crypt a humongous marble carved coffin held court, the face of a young lady with blonde hair halfway down her backside and a bouquet of roses in her hands carved on the coffin lid. Flora checked to make sure it would not open, but it was so heavy she couldn't have budged it, even if she wanted to get inside. And she didn't. She lay the painter's tarp down on the cool floor and rolled herself up in it for the night, her feet facing the doorway so she would see anyone if they tried to come in beside her. She shivered and cried silent tears as she lay there listening to the wind warring above the clouds and the hum of the freeway traffic intermingled with the constant sirens. And then there was nothing.

***

Flora opened her eyes, looking around with caution as she let the painter's tarp slide from her shoulders. Her feet, still sliced by broken glass, ached as she stood up and brushed her hair from her face. She peeked out of the crypt door. It was dusk in the cemetery. They'd have to watch for the cemetery caretaker, but this historical cemetery stayed open 24/7. Stepping out into the watery blue light, she stretched, noticing a ragged hole in her left wing. It didn't hurt much, thankfully. Flora began to walk amongst the tombstones in the older part of the cemetery. It was her favorite part of the cemetery because of all the tall elms and oaks and the carpet of bluebells that blanketed the ground in early spring. She smiled as she watched a squirrel scamper up a tree. The air held the musty, earthen smoke smell always there after a fire. Pan. She didn't see him amongst the graves or resting on a marble park bench or passed out beneath a tree. She checked every crypt door. They were all locked tight. A stone grew in Flora's throat. She choked back her tears. She would not cry. Pan would come today. And she would wait.

***

It had been two sunrises and Flora slowly accepted the fact that Pan was not coming. He didn't get out of the warehouse fire and she was alone. *Alone* is a terror word that takes hold of your gut and shakes it. Flora had never lost anyone, never been alone. She felt the wolf of fear nipping at her heels and stayed herself against a tree to keep from screaming as tears dripped off her nose. A funeral was going on and Flora decided since she had no way to say goodbye to her friend, Pan, she would witness this burial and say goodbye to him. She hid behind a massive tree trunk, petting the bark to soothe herself and keep her from crying out.

She watched a large group of humans dressed in all the colors of a garden approach a white casket with ornate silver handles that glinted in the sun. She'd never seen this type of funeral, but she liked it. Celebrating life and color, not death. Many of the women carried fans with a man's face on them or parasols to protect them. The men wore suits and ties, some wearing matching hats. A tall, important looking man in a black dress with a white collar stood at the head of the casket with an open book. Flora could not hear what he said, but she dared not get any closer. Women wailed and stomped their feet. The men bared witness in stoic silence, their hats held at their waists, the sun beaming on their gleaming heads. And then a woman in purple approached the man in the black dress. They shook hands. The woman opened her mouth and Flora heard the most beautiful bird song she ever heard on this planet. The woman sang, "Amazing grace, how sweet the sound that saved a wretch like me…" The notes floated high above the treetops and all the birds were silent. Flora cried as she listened. She hoped Pan found his own amazing grace. She wasn't quite sure what that was, but it sounded like a powerful and peaceful place to rest.

A metal cranking sound broke the perfect beauty of the moment and the white casket began to lower itself, as if by magic. The crowd of mourners passed by single file and threw flowers on top of the deceased human. And then they all left. Flora, alone again, found a shady spot to sit, crossed her knees, picked a blade of glass to twirl in her hands, and contemplated the ritual she just observed, wondering if Pan would appreciate it.

She was not aware of what time it was, but the sun had crept higher in the sky. Bees buzzed in the honeysuckle row against the fence. Her stomach rumbled as she watched a stranger approach, a male human in worn jeans with a funny crest of pink hair shooting up from the top of his head. It reminded her of a woodpecker. Pan explained this style was called a "mohawk." Did that mean the man was part hawk, part bird? Could he fly like her?

Flora darted behind a stand of old trees and peeked with one eye around a trunk. The man sat down on a bench facing one of the gravestones. He opened a paper bag and took out a white box. He opened the box and munched on some type of folded food in white paper. Flora's nose wrinkled at the hot spice of it. The man ate three of those folded wraps. She watched tiny green shredded vegetation fall from the wraps onto the bench. He drank something out of a tall red metal can and then searched for a place to throw away his garbage. Flora ducked back behind the treeline. She waited until the man walked to the front of the cemetery and then counted to one hundred just to be sure, before she raced to the wire wastebasket and dug out the bag the man tossed inside. She opened it. The smell of something fishy and spicy hit her. There was a small part of one of the folded white foods left. She reached into the bag and lifted it to her open mouth. She grimaced and spat it out. It was not sweet, and it tasted of death and emptiness. Flora ran to one of the water pumps to rinse the bad taste out of her mouth and went searching for fresh nectar among the flowers in the cemetery.

***

For the next few weeks, the man with the hawk hair came every Wednesday when the sun was high in the sky. He always brought the same food, and Flora would watch from behind the safety of the trees. Once, she thought she was spotted when he seemed to glance her way and pause in midbite, but then the small square thing he carried on him chirped and he turned his attention away. She breathed a sigh of relief and crept further back into the shadows.

After the man left that Wednesday—Flora knew it was Wednesday because the groundskeepers always talked about the strange man—Flora decided to go observe the construction of the new baseball stadium. (Apparently, Wednesday marked some part of the turning of the sun and how humans measured their time.)

On the highest hill of the cemetery stood an abandoned church, which Flora explored many times and, finding nothing of interest, she grew bored. Crosses dotted the hill like tiny growing trees. A lot of humans were buried on that hill. It took a long time to climb the winding cement steps and when Flora reached the top and walked around to the back of the church, she was out of breath, her spiracles on her side moving quite fast. She closed her eyes and swayed with the sound of the leaves blowing in the wind. It seemed unusually windy on this Wednesday afternoon. The construction site was busy. Flora could hear men shouting orders. She watched for a while and then headed down the hill to her favorite part of the cemetery.

***

It was Wednesday again and the man with the hawk hair was late. Flora sat near a child's grave, resting her head on the lamb statue and closed her eyes. Her body went rigid, her tongue slid in and out of her mouth quicker than a hummingbird's flight. Her eyes flickered and her body jittered. She moaned, a bit of white foam leaking from one corner of her mouth. Her head felt like it was being repeatedly hit with a dense piece of wood. She pressed her palms against the earth and felt the steady *tha-wump! tha-wump!* of her heartbeat. Her face to the sky, images flashed across the screen of her eyelids—men in hard hats arguing, steel toed boots, a great wrenching and grinding shriek, as if the Tree of Life itself fell to the ground and the earth shook as clouds of dust rose from the construction site. Men lay broken and bleeding, unmoving. Her eyes jerked open. Oh no! Big Blue was going to crash! She had to warn the men!

She flew as fast as she could, not worried about her safety as she hovered above the giant crane. The men on the ground looked like tiny marching ants. She could hear them screaming and pointing, taking shiny things out of their pockets and gesturing towards her.

Flora swallowed and steeled herself. She lowered herself to the crane. Its blue metal was hot on her bare feet. "Please! There is going to be an accident!"

The men on the ground screamed and ran away from her. Frustrated, Flora's eyes flashed bright in the sun, her antennae quivering in frustration, her wings stretched boldly behind her, dark moss green and rippling with the increasing force of the wind. Her antennae became to hum with the vibration of Big Blue's shaking cobalt mass and then a roaring rang in her ears so loud, she felt blood running down her cheek and Flora was tumbling head over heels, unable to control her descent because the force of the gust of wind was too great for her delicate wings. Dust filled her mouth and nostrils. She landed heavily on a folded mass of steel girders with a stabbing pain in her side. Glancing down, she saw a metal rod jammed in her left side. It had punctured a spiracle. Struggling for breath amongst the dust, sirens, and commotion, Flora gritted her teeth and pulled her body inch by screaming inch from the metal that pinned her to the wreckage that was now Big Blue. Men's screams and the coming sirens were muffled by her damaged ears.

She managed to stumble away from the crash without anyone noticing, for who would notice a Mothgirl amidst the accident? It was only after, when humans had the time to recall the tragedy on live television for the reporters that some would remember her standing atop the massive structure, her wings whipping about in the blustery afternoon.

With great effort, Flora made her way across the freeway before the traffic jam of emergency vehicles and dragged herself over the chain-link fence. Her chest felt like a volcano gushing with every breath. Her ears rang. Her vision blurry, her corneas scratched with grey dust from the collapse, she staggered to her favorite spot in the cemetery and lay beneath her favorite trees to say goodbye to this wonderful planet. She lost consciousness for a few minutes and when her eyelids flickered open a large shadow loomed over her, his head encompassed by a halo of sunlight, his pink mohawk the color of impatiens in July. It was him, the man who came alone to the cemetery every Wednesday to eat tacos.

Flora grimaced and struggled to sit up, but she could not. She pressed a hand to her injured side. It felt hot.

The man knelt beside her like one of the statues in the cemetery. His eyes were the color of her favorite bluebells. When he smiled, laugh lines appeared. "Don't move. You're hurt." He stared at her in utter wonder. "I'm Michael."

"Flora," she whispered as quiet as a flea.

Michael took off his navy windbreaker and laid it on top of the shivering creature. She was a miracle. He had never seen anything like her before, but he had read about the Mothman. He didn't know Mothgirl existed, though. But she did. He grinned and shook his head. "I'm sorry. How can I help you?"

"W-water?" Flora's voice crackled like straw in autumn beneath his feet.

He glanced around and saw the pump. "I'll be right back."

A few minutes later he came to her with one of those tall red cans filled with water. He supported the back of her head so she could drink. She winced and he noticed a line of dried blood running from her eardrum.

"Thank you." She lay her head back down and closed her eyes.

"Can I get someone to help you?"

"No. There is no one on your planet that can help me." Flora pulled the windbreaker from her puncture wound and Michael saw how hard she struggled to breathe, the round holes on her sides vibrating faster and faster.

"There must be someone," he said.

"Don't go." Flora grabbed his large hand with hers. "Stay with me until the end."

"Okay." The man stared down at her throat, so slender and beautiful. "Is there anything I can do to make you more comfortable?"

"Yes," she whispered. "Do you know the song 'Amazing Grace'?"

"I do," he said. And he began to sing.

ABOUT THE AUTHOR

Nora B. Peevy is a syndicate author for *Thrill Ride eZine* and The Butchered Writers. She is an editor for Baynam Books Press. She also is a freelance narrator and editor. *For the Sake of Brigid*, her first novelette, came out on May 24, 2024 from Baynam Books Press, and her first short story collection, *Cemetery Tacos and Other Delights,* is being published in April 2026 by Trepidatio. Her debut novel, *Flesh-Eating Turtles!* was published in June 2025 by The Evil Cookie Publishing. Her story "What's in Her Pimple?" made *The Best of Carnage House: Year One 2025*. She also reads scripts for the H.P. Lovecraft Film Festival.

www.ingramcontent.com/pod-product-compliance
Lightning Source LLC
LaVergne TN
LVHW051004080826
845145LV00009B/2450

9781685101725